A FLOATING WORLD

Stories

by Karen Best

Published 2012 by Beating Windward Press LLC

For contact information, please visit:
www.BeatingWindward.com

Copyright © Karen D. Best, 2012
All Rights Reserved
Cover Design: Copyright © House of Thuan, 2012
Book Design: Copyright © KP Creative, 2012

First Edition
ISBN: 978-0-9838252-1-0

To Jeanne Leiby
for encouraging impractical pursuits.

Eternity in Ice

Snowflakes spiraled out of a leaden sky, dusting the shoulders of Gwen's jacket. Kevin spun on his skates, his leather jacket made a creaking noise as his arms flailed. He laughed, displaying sharp white teeth.

Gwen could not help but share his exuberance. Amsterdam had been hazy and dark. They wasted nights getting high in run-down bars. The scents of smoke and heavy perfume sticking to her exposed skin in a vinyl booth as two shiny meat androids fucked. Kevin laughing in a bitter way, Gwen pressing her cheek against a filmy tabletop. Now that they were in Stockholm, she was feeling better. The air was clear and cool, the afternoon pleasantly dim, as if the light were leaking in from some other dimension. She took Kevin's hand and let him spin her on her unsteady skates.

"What do you want to do later, babe?" he asked.

"Buy something stupid," she said.

"Like what?"

"Whatever. Some tourist bullshit." She wobbled, but he caught her.

"Whoa. Remember, balance."

"Right, sorry. Let me sit a minute." She skated over to a wooden bench that was off to the side of the frozen pond.

"This is so Old World, isn't it?" Kevin put his arm around her. The bench was freezing, but at least it was stable. Gwen rubbed her gloved hands together. A powder of white was settling in her hair and eyelashes, prismatic through the sun's rays. Graceful Swedes skated elegantly past them. Two girls in matching pink parkas, puffy as two sugar-coated marshmallows, giggled at them. Across the pond, on another bench under a spindly tree, three huge Viking guys in black leather passed around a flask and scowled.

"I'm cold. Why'd we come here again?"

"To see the world. What kind of writer could I be otherwise?"

"One that actually writes?"

"Gwen, I told you, I'm not starting my novel until we get home. Right now, I just want to experience and absorb it all."

"Whatever, sweetheart." The big metalhead guys seemed to be staring at them. Gwen wished she had worn an extra pair of stockings. Her legs were feeling very cold and weak. One of the guys jumped down from the bench and crouched by the edge of the pond. He let his long platinum hair fall over his face very theatrically. One of the others punched him in the back and handed him the flask.

Kevin had that pensively disgusted look he got whenever he and Gwen argued; looking high up into the sky and chewing his lower lip.

"It's too cold to sit still. I'm going to keep skating."

"Kev." Gwen grabbed his arm. Beneath all the layers of clothing, he felt like a mannequin, without the give of flesh. "Don't be mad."

"I'm not mad."

"Would you get me a hot chocolate?"

"In a minute." He skated away.

She had never been this cold before in her life. Even her guts chattered. She looked forward to going back to their hotel room, burrowing under the sheets with Kevin, feeling his warm skin against her, his scent of patchouli, having enough vodka to keep them warm through the night. A hot bath, with so much steam the mirror would be lost in fog.

The surly-looking metalheads were all standing now, in a military line. Whatever they were waiting for, it had arrived. And Gwen saw her.

A tall girl in a black fur coat and an elaborately ruffled black skirt, long blue dreadlocks piled on her head, glided past them. Their scowls melted into a look of peace, almost religious or orgasmic. They watched her with the unguarded hunger of a pack of wolves. For her part, she slid easily through the blonde teenage girls and clumsily bundled boys, never looking at anyone.

She was locked in her own self, her face a gorgeous icon from the pages of a magazine. Her skates were shiny and black, with gleaming sharp blades. Gwen chewed a flake of purple paint off her nail. It was engulfed by the white snow the instant she spat it onto the ground. A splinter of blind jealousy pricked her.

She skated over to the rental booth and removed her skates. The man behind the counter handed over her boots. She would get her own damn hot chocolate. From the window of the corner coffee shop Gwen watched Kevin circling the pond. He slipped and slid at least two feet on the ice, nearly knocking over the blue-haired girl. Gwen laughed to herself, waiting for the line to advance. She made sure she had enough money, paid for her drink and dumped extra cinnamon into it. Across the street, Kevin was now leaning on the girl, laughing. That same guilty laugh he used when his pathetic lies failed. She imagined his *Damn, someone must have tripped me* in the face of this obviously unimpressed Swedish girl. She flicked some snow off his shoulder, her arm around his waist. He took a step back and brushed at the wet snow still clinging to his pants. The girl's feet were set at an angle to each other, like a ballet dancer's. She clasped her hands behind her back and spoke to him. Then she put out her hand, which Kevin accepted.

The three guys had been watching the exchange, and now one of them was snarling, his lip curled back over wolf-white teeth. She was probably just being friendly. Gwen hoped one of the Viking guys would play jealous boyfriend and intervene. She wanted to believe that Kevin was being friendly, but he was holding her arm gently. He'd touched Gwen in a perverse multitude of ways, but never with such reverence. Kevin and the girl were transfixed by each other, a look of secretive knowing on both their faces. They didn't even watch where they were going. Gwen gulped her drink, winced as the scalding liquid hit flowed into her stomach.

"Kev," she shouted, standing far enough from the pond not to slip on the ice. He did not respond. They moved over to the booth, the girl seating herself on a bench as Kevin kneeled and removed her skates.

3

"Kevin, didn't you hear me?"

"I'm sorry."

"Well next time..."

"Do I know you?" Kevin's eyebrows drew together in confusion.

Gwen thought she was supposed to laugh, but was too afraid. "Whatever. As I was saying..."

"I'm sorry, you must think I'm someone else." He returned to undoing the laces on the girl's skates. She sat on the bench, indifferently watching the tourists argue.

"Okay, shut up now. This isn't funny anymore."

"I don't know who you're looking for, but it's not me."

"Cut it out." She grabbed his arm. Her hand trembled.

"Please, I don't know you. Leave us be," he said, removing her hand.

"Kevin, stop. You're really pissing me off."

"I don't know you." He placed the girl's skates in a shiny black bag and helped her into her other boots. The girl yawned.

"Stop it. This is stupid. Kevin."

"I'm sorry, darling," he said to the blue-haired girl. She only looked away.

"Who the hell is this, anyway?"

"Just ignore her," Kevin said. He stood and slid his arm around the girl's waist.

"You'd better not fucking ignore me. Kevin. Goddamn it." Gwen glanced over her shoulder. People were looking. She hoped that the three tall black leather guys would do something now. They were so blatant about watching that girl. But they stood there. Kevin and the girl turned and began walking down the street. Gwen's fingers dug into the paper cup.

"Fuck you." She threw the hot chocolate onto the ground. It steamed against the snow, melting it.

She walked around the pond to where the three men stood.

"Hey, what's going on?"

The one in the middle, the white-haired one, scowled. One of the others tapped him on the arm, and they walked away.

"Damn it, I'm talking to you," she shouted at their backs.

This was a stupid joke. That girl, she'd watched it all so smugly, her little eyebrows arched up in amusement. Gwen wished she'd thrown her drink on that bitch's little goth dolly get-up. That would stop her from smirking. A flare of anger licked at her stomach. When she got a hold of Kevin, she'd show him what a mistake he'd made.

As she marched back to the hotel, she mentally flipped through Kevin's belongings, trying to select one to burn. Once again, she wished he'd started his novel already so she could burn that, but she settled for his sex show photos from Amsterdam.

Once inside the hotel lobby, she was relieved by the universality of the place. The sun streamed in through huge glass windows etched by frost. Businessmen and women waited in the tastefully oversized white chairs. This hotel lobby could be anywhere, could be down the street from home, where her mother hovered over the phone waiting for her call. Gwen pushed this thought away, kept if from dampening her anger. She rode the elevator to the third floor and walked down to her room. A group of Americans passed her, talking loudly in the hall. She thrust her key into the lock, twisting it so hard it hurt her hand.

The lock did not give. She jiggled the key, checked the numbers, twisted harder and harder until a red imprint of the key was left in the flesh of her fingers. She kicked the door, cursed, breathed deeply, but the lock was unmoved.

"Hi, I'm in room 340, and my key isn't working."

The desk clerk blinked her huge mascaraed eyelashes. "Name?"

"Gwen Scott."

The clerk looked into her computer screen, her face blank. "I'm sorry. We don't have that."

"Shit. It's probably under Ronson. Kevin."

"No, sorry. That room is empty."

"What?"

"340 is not rented. Neither of those names are in here."

"Jesus. Listen, I just checked in yesterday."

"I'm sorry."

"I don't care. I just want to get into my room."

"I'm sorry," The counter girl's beige lips turned downward.

"Please." Gwen gripped the edge of the polished counter tightly.

"I'm sorry."

Gwen pulled herself up straight. She would go walk about a bit, then come back. Kevin would be back. He would straighten everything out. She thanked the clerk, aware that she should be absolutely screaming at the mascaraed lady. When Kevin came back, then the screaming would commence.

A powdery snow fell. Small, shiny cars crept by on the slushy street. The sky settled onto the world, a vaulted ice cathedral, dripping and blocking out the light. One of the reasons Kevin had wanted to come here was the long night.

At a small store with creaky wooden floors, she bought herself a black scarf and wrapped it around her neck, caressing the edge of it as she walked. Her legs ached and her boots were caked with frozen mud. It was getting darker. Gwen wondered how deep the nights could get here. The stars were luminous here, so different from the heavy sky back home in Florida, where they flickered dispassionately.

Kevin would come back, he had to. Otherwise she might be stuck here. Kevin would return and save her from making that call to her mother, pleading *You were right about him. Please bring me home.*

It was after midnight. She'd spent as long as she dared in the lobby, waiting. According to the clerk, a different one this time, room 340 was still unoccupied. Gwen counted the creased travelers checks in her pocket. Not enough for even one night. Kevin had most of their money. They were traveling on what he'd inherited when his father died.

She was hungry and exhausted. She had a glass of wine and vegetable lasagna in the hotel restaurant. After that, there was very little of her money left. Once security started circling around her, she went out again.

A blur of cafes, late-night clubs, straight sidewalks that lead nowhere reeled around her. She stayed in a club where they played loud, sugary pop music long enough to spend half of what she had left on a watered down vodka tonic and dig some speed out of her purse, so she would not drop from exhaustion right there.

The morning came in gritty gray tones. Gwen's stomach complained. The hunger and the speed's aftereffects made her want to vomit. It was cold. She was short for the tea she ordered, but the young, pierced guy behind the counter let it go. She drank as slowly as possible, mentally composing her speech to her mother. Gwen could just hear the voice coming over the phone line. *What were you thinking? I told you, you're too young to go running around with some guy to godknowswhere. I want you to remember this, Gwendolyn. I warned you about that boy.*

There had to be another way to get home.

She had no idea where she was. The pocket map folded in the bottom of her purse was useless, a mass of lines and unpronounceable names that had no significance anymore. Her face sweated from the speed, her entire body felt dirty, her hair heavy with the snow and grime. The numbness in her fingers had metamorphosed almost into a burning sensation. One narrow street squeezed into to another. She had to be miles from the hotel by now. Old apartment buildings pressed on her from the right and left, all the windows not quite square, all the angles off by a few degrees. The ground beneath her tilted. She commanded her legs to move, but they could not. Gwen attempted to grab the low gate she was standing in front of to steady herself. She felt her limbs go liquid, and blackness swallowed her.

Someone was talking to her. It was her mother, saying to get up, that she was not too sick to go to school. Gwen blinked away her mother's voice, and realized the one speaking was the woman in the black turtleneck standing over her.

"What happened?"

"Oh, you speak English?"

"Did I get hurt?"

"Other than a few bruises, no. You were outside my building. I let you in."

Gwen pulled back the thick blanket and tried to sit up. A wave of vertigo pushed her back.

"No. Lie down."

"Thank you," she said.

"My name is Lux. What happened to you?"

"I'm lost," she said.

"You're far from home?"

"I need to find someone."

"You can tell me later. Now drink this." She gave Gwen a steaming mug of something greenish and slightly bitter-smelling. "Tastes bad, but it will help you feel better."

She awoke feeling as if she'd slept for a thousand years. The room she was in was painted pale blue, with no furniture except for the futon she rested on and a sleek, all metal desk holding a grey computer. Gwen found the bathroom, where everything was pure white, even the rug, then wandered out into the living room.

Lux crouched in front of a covered hutch with a few rabbits inside. She was sticking carrots in through the mesh with her slender fingers. Her short, spiky black hair barely brushed the top of her grey sweater.

"Oh, you're up." She brushed off her hands and petted the hutch. "I was feeding them."

"How long did I sleep?"

"Two days," Lux shrugged.

"Fuck. Oh. Sorry."

"Do you know that if you don't have dreams, you die?"

"I hadn't heard that."

"Oh, it's very true. Come in, let's have lunch."

Over a bowl of hot beef stew, Gwen told Lux about Kevin's grand plan to see Europe and write his great novel.

"And what is the story?"

"It's some dumb thing about a guy who fucks his way around Europe. Kev likes to think he's going to be the next Marquis de Sade or Anaïs Nin. You know, so controversial, exploding taboos, all that junk. Last he told me, he was calling it 'Sex Thieves'." Gwen dunked a piece of hard bread into her stew.

"I don't understand. Sex thieves?"

"It doesn't make sense to me, either."

"Where did you lose him?"

"On a pond. We were skating, and this girl came up. She had lots of blue hair. Dressed up like some Victorian widow. Anyway, I went to get a drink, and the next thing, Kevin was unlacing her skates and saying he didn't know me."

"Oh no."

"I couldn't even go back to the hotel."

"This woman, did she have a group of men following her? Tall men, wearing black with long hair?"

"Yeah." Gwen stopped eating.

"Thora."

"Is that her name?"

"You may never get your Kevin back. And if you do, he won't be the same person."

"What the hell are you talking about?"

"Thora. She's bad. She does this all the time."

"How do you know?"

Lux rose from the table and took Gwen by the wrist, leading her into a room; the only place in the house that was not pale and minimalist. The walls were covered with photos, some of people, but most of old ruins. The bed was covered in a lush plum velvet comforter. Precious counter space was occupied by silver jewelry boxes, half-burned lavender candles and short stacks of forgotten items; pens, empty bottles, a bee encased in a lucite cube. Lux sat cross-legged in front of a dresser. She pulled a drawer open and dug through the contents. Her hand snapped out, holding an old photo. The corner was torn off, but it was clearly Lux, standing next to a boy with long, shiny platinum hair. He had his arm around her, and was smiling. They appeared to be standing in front of the apartment building.

"Did you see him? A man who looks like this? Tall, black leather jacket. Did you?" She held the photo inches from Gwen's face.

"Yeah, yeah. I saw him."

Lux let out a wounded sigh and pressed the picture against the floor, covering his face with her outstretched fingers.

"Varick. He was my lover, until he saw her. He ran towards her, out of a crowd. He never came home."

"What does this mean?"

"Go back home. Forget about Kevin. He's gone."

"I can't do that." Gwen turned. She had to get away for a minute. This was all too bizarre to believe. Maybe if she went back to sleep. "Tell me where she is."

"That will get you nothing. Do you want to see him spit on you, push you away?"

"This is crazy. Why am I in this crazy fucking country? If you know where Kevin might be, I want you to show me." Gwen braced herself against the doorway. Lux slumped on the floor, the photo still under her hand.

"You're so young. I want to help."

"If you really wanted to help, you'd take me."

"Not tonight. Tomorrow." Lux wiped the tears from under her eyes with the backs of her hands.

"More?" Lux asked. Gwen nodded and her glass was topped off with brandy. Lux sat across from her on the couch. Two of the rabbits were sniffing her bare feet. Her hair was crushed flat on one side, where she'd rested her cheek against the arm.

"Varick was always so quiet. At first I thought he didn't want to tell me why. Everyone seemed to know who Thora was, but no one was friends with her."

The two candles on the table between them flickered. Lux gathered her legs underneath herself.

"I finally saw them together. I asked him to come home. He acted so insulted. For a few minutes, I thought I must have done something. A clue was missing. Then I thought, no, everyone at least deserves an explanation."

"Did you ever get one?"

Lux laughed. "No. I tried to sort it out, in my dreams. I looked for other people who she'd taken them from. They all told the same story. Their lovers, good or bad, had run away to her, and wouldn't talk to them."

"She couldn't have even said that much to him." Gwen looked down into her glass. The candlelight flickered through the bronze liquid. "And then what happens?"

"When?"

"When she's finished with them?"

"You saw how they followed her. Even my Varick. Still drawn to her."

"I think you're looking for him too." Gwen slid off the couch onto the floor. She pressed her finger into the pool of wax collecting under the candle.

"Sometimes, I think I hear the door opening. I think, Varick's finally come back. I'll be lying in bed, and I can't move, because I think that it might be real this time. I don't want to get up and see that it's not."

Gwen punctured the lukewarm skin of the wax and let the hot molten core run over her finger. It hardened there.

"The only theory I can give you," Lux said, "is that Thora somehow changes people. Varick was never cheerful, but after her, he became hateful. He enjoyed nothing. When I looked into his eyes, it was as if the soul was gone. Everything he saw, everything but Thora, was dirt, waste. All he could see was the ugliness."

"I won't let her take Kevin." Gwen peeled the wax off her fingers.

"I don't know how willing he is. Thora has no heart. That, itself, is a powerful force. People can imagine whatever they like about her. She can't prove them right or wrong. She can't disappoint anyone by not loving them, or loving them too much."

Gwen said nothing. She drank, and refilled her glass. She wondered what she could tell her mother when she got home. She'd quit school for this trip. How long until people started asking, *Where's Kevin? Why didn't he come home?*

"You don't have to go," Lux said. "You can stay with me. I'll make sure you get home." She knelt on the floor across from Gwen. The candles burned in their faces. Lux put both her hands on the tabletop.

"But I have to," Gwen said.

"I thought you'd say that."

"I'm sorry. I appreciate everything."

Lux silenced Gwen by pressing her fingers against Gwen's lips. "I wanted you to stay." Lux rose and put her glass in the kitchen. One candle burned itself out, expiring in a plume of smoke as Lux closed herself in her room.

The next afternoon, after a long, hungover sleep, they drove in silence, the evening deepening into those long dark nights. Lux's Volkswagen rumbled and leaked only a little heat. Gwen had showered and borrowed some clothes from Lux while hers were in the dryer. Lux drove, biting her lip so hard Gwen could see the edge of it turning red.

In the shower, she'd wept with relief, then with disgust at herself. She was going to get the money from him and go home. She would not demand an explanation. She would not let Thora see her break. Thora was her enemy, and now, she supposed, Kevin was too.

Lux pulled up against the curb in front of a square brick building, dropped like a sooty and careless block on the city.

"Second floor. That's hers. I won't go in, but I'll be here," Lux said.

Gwen got out and stepped carefully over the icy sidewalk to the rickety door. She rode the huge elevator up and knocked on the only door she saw. The wall looked newer, as if it had been added to the much older, flaking red brick building. A tiny window let her see Lux's car below.

A pain spread through her lungs, an underwater bursting sensation. Thora stood in the door, dressed in her ropes of blue hair and a white dress with a tall, swan-necked collar. Her face was blank, inaccessible. Her eyebrows were drawn in the same color as her hair, and her sharp, carved from ice cheeks were dusted with fine silver glitter.

"Kevin, please," Gwen said, regretting the submissive politeness in her voice.

"Come in," Thora said.

The space was a huge loft, a table and easel set up under one window, splatters of paint on the concrete floor underneath. Huge silver mirrors had been hung around the room, silver portals to alternate versions of the room, just as bare as the one in which Gwen stood. At a low glass-topped table in the center of the room, Kevin was bent over something, his plain, brown hair almost reaching his eyes. He was wearing a black button-down shirt with an old Sisters of Mercy t-shirt over top, a few shades lighter black.

"Kevin?" Gwen stood behind him. He grunted and continued to work. It was a board of something that looked like glass, with little glass cubes he was trying to arrange on the board. "I need to talk to you."

"What?"

Thora went out a narrow door onto the tiny fire escape. She lit a cigarette with a jeweled silver lighter. Gwen sat in the chair opposite Kevin.

"What's going on?"

Kevin stopped and looked up at her. "Are you disturbing me for a good reason?"

"You fuck. Stop pretending you don't know me."

"I think I might, but that doesn't matter." His brown eyes looked like the frosted windows, something dulling the reflected light there.

"What the hell does that mean?"

"I don't expect you to understand." He looked at her with

uncut contempt. Gwen wondered if there really was such a thing as the evil eye, because it felt like her insides were all shriveling and turning black. Gwen walked over to the door and squeezed out onto the balcony. Thora did not move. The cold was giving her face an eerie, porcelain-doll rouge.

"What did you do to him?"

"You are very pretty." Thora exhaled slowly. Smoke haloed her gorgeous face.

"Shut the fuck up. What did you do?"

"People could hate you for that." She reached out one black-clawed hand to stroke Gwen's face. Gwen batted her away.

"You did something. He won't even talk to me."

"I do nothing."

"You don't understand. I loved him. He loved me. I would never have come to this fucking stupid cold insane asylum anyway. You have to tell me."

"I am." She took a slow, elegant drag. "That is the answer." Gwen wanted to hit her, but realized that would do nothing. She would still be standing there, in the snow, a perfect glossy fantasy waiting to be filled by whatever imagination dragged itself toward her.

"What is? You haven't said anything."

"I told you, I don't do. I am just here."

"What does that have to do with Kevin?"

Thora shrugged.

"What did you tell him on the pond?"

"A secret." She smiled.

"I want some answers." Gwen crossed her arms.

"You Americans all think you're entitled to everything. What if I think you don't need an answer?"

"Someone needs to tell me something. I'm not leaving until it happens."

"Go home," she said, flicking her cigarette off the balcony. Gwen followed Thora inside.

"Listen, bitch. You think you can just…"

"I'm tired, Kevin, darling. Deal with this." Thora waved

her hand and retreated beyond a door.

Kevin rose and moved toward Gwen, an alien expression of hostility on his face. Gwen reached back and yanked his wallet out by the long chain.

"God, don't touch me," he yelled and twisted away from her. She emptied the wallet of money and threw it back on the table.

Gwen pressed her tongue hard against the roof of her mouth to swallow back the tears.

"You bastard. I hope your dick gets frostbite and falls off."

"I don't even know you, girl."

Gwen grabbed the glass board and smashed it against the floor. She knew it was nothing, it meant nothing, but she needed to smash something, and whatever had happened to Kevin, she could not smash that. She ran down the staircase to Lux's car.

On the way back, it snowed hard, the wind whipping ice against buildings and parked cars. Gwen's fist was still clenched around the money. She would never be able to tell anyone at home what had happened to her.

Gwen thought of Kevin and Varick and the countless others who had come to Thora like the snow presses itself against windowpanes. She imagined Kevin sitting with the others at the pond. It was snowing hard, the crystalline beauty of each snowflake a release from every passing face, every light, every gutter. Thora twirled on the frozen pond, circling herself. She was complete, orbiting her own internal star. They could not touch her. The men gathered into a circle, turning their backs to the wind as they sculpted, together, a human figure out of ice. Gwen saw them shaking like starving wolves in the snow.

Blizzard Season

They came with the first snowflakes of winter, emerging under pearly gray skies from the edges of empty parking lots and suburbs-to-be. Like an unassuming plant coming into bloom, they were suddenly everywhere. In a strip of untended land between the sidewalk and your apartment building—a place you couldn't even see anymore for having walked past every day—suddenly, a white hand parting the spindly branches. Hair as black as asphalt, lips like blood. No: stoplights. A girl shivering; lost, flinching. She clutches the leg of your pants as though you're the only person in the world that can help her. You think she's the victim of a crime and you offer to take her down to the police station. She's going on and on about a huntsman and you have no idea what she could mean by that but her clothes are torn and her hands on your legs are freezing. At least you can get her a cocoa and stay with her until she calms down enough to make sense, so you take her arm and walk with her to a coffee shop. It's only once you calm her down enough that she can sit down and assure her that the cocoa isn't some sort of potion that you notice she's dressed like she's going to the Renaissance festival. And like that, they appeared all over the city.

No one knew where they came from, or even how many there were. Could have just been a gang of waifish runaways, except they all told the same story. A wicked stepmother, a magic mirror. They were terrified of apples. It was not clear what name would be used to refer to them. Some people liked *Snows* and some liked *Grimm Girls* and those of a literary bent used *Märchen Mädchen*, the story girls.

So many of us had forgotten that this story wasn't all sweet little birds that helped wash your dishes and cheery songs and princes on white horses. The girls came from a world of soot and straw and iron shoes. The one you'd found, that you calmed with cocoa and your jacket, went home with you like a stray kitten. You were raised right, so you let her have your bed while you slept on the couch. In the morning, you found her crouched in front of the open refrigerator weeping in confusion over bags of salad and packaged cheese slices. Water pouring from the faucet made her leap back, repelled. You didn't even want to consider what would happen if you turned on the TV. To make her feel better, you decided to offer her some clean clothes. Her gown was dirty and ripped in a way that inspired the same impure thoughts you used to have about the St. Pauli Girl. You found some clothes that your ex-girlfriend left behind when she moved to Portland. She giggled at the jeans and called them *breeches*. As she tentatively poked at the miniblinds, you wondered how she was ever going to survive.

Well-meaning men on television talked about shelters, blankets, and a moratorium on mirrors. Police tried to find out where they came from and never got any answers. Special houses were opened for the influx of traumatized girls. Informally, they were known as Snow Houses. Men who worked nearby just happened to reroute their paths to carry them past the Snow Houses when the girls were out walking in the yard, because one thing that was true about them was that each one was the fairest in the land, and even when you thought you'd seen the prettiest girl, the next one would be inexpressibly more beautiful. But if you walked past a Snow House at midnight, you'd see furtive faces at the windows, hear voices in unison whimpering.

The reformers wanted to heal them of their trauma. Workshops were held, refugees invited to talk about their stepmothers and invite their spirits to heal through shamanistic dance therapy. People who called talk radio shows said the girls were all drains on the system, and why couldn't they just get jobs instead of asking for government handouts? One group countered with the proposal that what the city needed was an influx of wicked stepmothers. Weren't there hundreds, if not thousands, of incomplete stories out there now? Stacks of glass coffins, empty? Princes riding around in circles? Auditions were held. Wanted: Stern ladies with aristocratic bearing. Joan-Crawford-style eyebrows a plus. A concert was put on to benefit the refugees. An internet rumor went around that the refugees were a hoax organized by crazed Grimm Brothers fans. Black hair dye and red lipstick sold out in drugstores. One girl was pelted with apples until she fell into the gutter. There was talk of a movie deal.

The refugees spilled out of the city's charitable institutions. Some wandered the streets, offering, for a few coins, to do fine needlework or spin wool. They all had skills no one needed anymore. You might have heard that some people would take a girl home and make her mop the floors. It was said that the girls were good at drudgery, and all they ever seemed to want in exchange were crusts of bread and anonymity. Before spring, a few of them even walked to the school bus, though by then it was hard to tell by looking which girls were genuine and which one were imitators. The ones who did go to school were even more lost than before. They were pretty and polite, but they couldn't do math. Their handwriting was a labored mess of peaks and flourishes. They didn't know who Sir Isaac Newton was. They brought meat pies for lunch.

You tried to help the one you found get a place to stay, but the Snow Houses were overcrowded and you knew she had nowhere else, so you let her stay. It wouldn't have been right to make her go back onto the street. Some of the things you'd heard were too awful to contemplate. Better to let the huntsman cut out her heart than see her end up like some of the *Mädchen* did. It made your stomach hurt to know what people would do with a beautiful girl they were sure no one would ever look for. But she grew restless just sitting in your apartment all day. And you grew tired of explaining for the nth time, with the picture of your ex-girlfriend in your hand, that you hadn't painted a picture of your ex; that there were these things called *cameras* and they made *photographs*, while she nodded her pretty head.

When the snow started to go, so did they. If you were lucky, you might see one pushing her way back through the brambles. She might stop and look back at you—the wet streets, the hulking bus roaring away from the curb—as if waiting for you to put out your hand and take her cold fingers. But you wouldn't, and once the twigs closed behind her you would lose her oilslick-black hair in the darkness under the trees. And then you'd turn around and realize that you just missed your bus.

Thread

Justin was on the deck, leaning over the rail as he lowered a camera into the water. The slight breeze pressed his blue plaid shirt against his side. The air carried the salty decayed scent of the ocean and Miranda took a deep breath, ignoring the stab of pain in her gut. Her seasickness lingered. The boat rocked under her feet. She held the railing to steady herself.

"Did you sleep all right?"

"I guess. Still feeling kind of sick." The camera disappeared into the water, a black rubber cord snaking after it.

The awkwardness of being with Justin again had not yet worn off. He'd left their home in Florida two months ago to come to Iceland as part of a big documentary project funded by an assortment of environmental groups. It had something to do with all the trash in the oceans. Miranda had just gotten used to being alone in the house when he surprised her with a ticket to Reykjavik.

On the first day there had been the alien rock formations of the coast, clusters of black pillars stretching out into the ocean, the volcanic sands of the shores, glittering and dark. It looked like the beginning of the world—or the end. Treeless. Monochrome. Primitive lichens crawling across the boulders, turning them slowly to sand. Now, after three days at sea, there was just the monotonous expanse of charcoal sea and ashy sky. The two seemed to exchange colors for a few brief hours around midnight. Only the horizon gave any indication of the boundary between them. Patches of shocking green moss splayed over the rocky terrain. And down in the inlets, chunks of white ice floated in the water.

"Have some oatmeal. That might help," Justin said.

Miranda held on to his wrist, which seemed to have absorbed the hardness of the steel railing. She realized that he was not looking at her, but at the expanse of ocean over her right shoulder. Her fingers itched in the thick woolen gloves. The boat lurched again, and her stomach dropped. She tightened her grip to keep from slipping.

"There's a forest of kelp underneath us right now," Justin said, looking down into the water. Miranda tried to see under the undulating glassy surface of the ocean. The ocean was opaque as steel. "There's one spot in the ocean where all the junk that people dump gets caught up in the currents. Old fishing nets, plastic, medical waste too, probably." Justin pulled his wrist away so he could get out his camera. He aimed it at a seagull flying overhead. "It gets pushed together into one huge mass of garbage, and when fish go into it they get stuck and suffocate. Birds eat the garbage, too, and then they die because they think they're full of food, when really it's all plastic. They starve."

"Where is it?"

"Not too far. We're not there yet." Justin said.

Sunlight gilded the ocean. Miranda wondered how far it was to the bottom, and what was hiding there, among the ribbons of kelp.

She had wanted to tell him before they left the airport. But when he appeared, his eager smile and the unselfconscious dorkiness of his old Megadeth t-shirt under his jacket, the beat-up Converse on his feet worn to near transparency in spots reminded her of his daily emails and entreaties to come see him. She had imagined herself getting off the plane, telling him all about Peter. She would face her fate, she thought, though the idea was really more dramatic than necessary. She would exchange her plane ticket for one that departed as soon as possible. She owed it to him to do it in person. She'd never felt like she was herself with him, she might write later in an email once she'd gotten home. It was as if she'd been cast in a role of his design, not able to speak her own words. He never really knew her. And though she wasn't leaving him to be with Peter, she hoped the revelation would force Justin to see her differently; to see, after all, that she wasn't there to be the face in his viewfinder.

He destroyed her plan by saying *You don't know how much I've needed to see you* and clinging to her as though he might drown if he let go.

While Justin had been gone, he faded from Miranda's perceptions. No more underpants all over the floor. No more searching for something to dry herself with after a shower because he'd thrown the last clean towel, sopping wet, on the living room rug. No more Iron Maiden videos or dull stoner friends from film school or lectures about the way the dust produced when she filed her nails got everywhere or half-formed plans to save the world scribbled on torn sheets of notebook paper crumpling under the legs of the computer chair. She pushed his boxes of Transformers and warped cassette tapes to the back of the closet. Finally, Miranda had just herself and her work.

Miranda set her bowl of instant oatmeal and water in the microwave and pushed the button to turn it on. The ship needed more lights, and it carried a lingering smell of fish. While the machine whirred, she removed her gloves and flexed her hands, hoping to relieve some of the soreness in her fingers.

"Your mate tells me you are an artist," a man said. It was Halldor, the ship's captain. He stood in the doorway, his arms crossed as he leaned against the frame. The rust spotting the doorframe was the same color as the hair that poked from beneath his knit cap, ferrous and glinting like wire. His teeth were white as glaciers and straight. The coppery scruff on his face only made his teeth glow whiter.

"I don't know."

"What do you mean?"

"I'm working on something."

He stood next to her and reached for the coffeemaker, his arm just fractions of an inch from her face. The smell coming from him was of harsh soap and cigarettes. He stepped away to fill the pitcher with water.

"What kind of art, I mean," he said over the water.

"Oh, it's a tapestry."

"You mean a rug?"

"No, it hangs on a wall."

"But made with, yarn, or something?"

"Yes." The microwave chimed and she reached for her oatmeal. The chunky brown texture was unappealing, but Miranda stuck her spoon into it and stirred. She sat down and carefully scraped some of the oatmeal off her spoon with her front teeth.

The tapestry was bigger than the wall of the room where Miranda kept it. She rolled it up as she worked on it, so that only the unfinished edges were visible at once. It illustrated the Babylonian story of Tiamat. Miranda had been adding to it for three years, working in strips of plastic cut from shopping bags. She spliced different colors of plastic together to get a shaded effect in the water and on the blue-black body of Tiamat, twisting the strips into thick yarn. Justin once told her that plastic lasts hundreds of years, even in the harshest environments; she thought that made it a perfect way to depict the origin of the world, in a material that would outlast them all. Her tapestry would persist just as myths do.

Since the tapestry was worked in segments, most people couldn't see the full image. She kept a sketch of the complete picture taped to her loom. Still, no one she'd ever shown the tapestry to had been able to connect the swaths of crinkled blue with the crest of the waves in the sketch. She secretly enjoyed that, having this vision she could unfurl before others that remained hers alone.

Halldor leaned back against the narrow cabinet while the coffeemaker gurgled. The Magnusson brothers made her itch for some absorbing, repetitive activity to do with her hands, like cutting and tying the strips of plastic. Halldor, with his constant grinning and endless good spirits, and the other one, Kristjan, who never spoke and often stared out into the ocean with no expression on his face at all. They communicated by some secret system unknown to her. Even though Halldor chatted constantly in Icelandic to his brother and the handful of crew members, he accepted Kristjan's silence as if it were as mundane was the deck beneath his boots. A few times, straining to understand Halldor, Miranda had felt herself caught in Kristjan's stare, which went beyond her, as though she were nothing more than another wave in a sea of so many. The ghost sensations of yarn slipped through her fingertips, and she wished that the threads would come together, locking into a final picture of the Magnusson brothers in which all the strands meant something.

"How long until it is done?"

"I'm not sure, really. It's hard to say." She rubbed her fingers on her jeans to rid them of the slipping yarn feeling. "I'm making it out of plastic bags. I have to cut and join the pieces into threads, then loom them together." She hoped this would satisfy him so she could be left alone. She disliked talking about something so personal with a stranger. Instead he sat down across from her. His hands, lightly brushed with fine blonde hairs, rested on either side of her bowl. She pulled back to give herself more space.

"Sounds cool." He went to check on the coffee pot.

"Don't you have to pilot the ship?"

"My brother is doing it. Some drink?" he asked, holding out a dented metal flask.

"It's still morning."

He pointed to the digital clock on the wall, which showed that it was six pm.

Miranda bit down on the tips of her fingers to calm the slipping yarn feeling. Halldor was unkempt, mostly. If he had a long hot bath and a shave and serious shampoo all at once a gorgeous creature would emerge. His straight, small nose and even white teeth made his a trustworthy face, though the eyes held much more. The rocking motion of the boat made her stomach turn. She stood up.

"You don't have to go. I could use someone to talk with. Come on, let's tell a story."

"What kind of story?"

"Whatever you like," he said. A shiny band of scar tissue encircling his wrist caught the faint light.

"Tell me what you're doing here," she said.

"I am not sleeping." He shrugged.

"Not that. I mean, out here in the ocean."

"In the summer, we take tourists out to see the seals. They like to take pictures. It's less dangerous in the summer. We make money."

"You and your brother?"

"Yes. He used to have his own boat."

"What happened?" Miranda leaned closer. She pressed her fingers to the tabletop. Now she was making him uncomfortable with her staring. She could see it in the way he crossed his arms. The oily surface of his coffee rippled with the motion of the boat.

"It went down into the sea some years ago. It was in the winter. A storm came up. He was swept into the water. The coast guard couldn't rescue anyone because of the storm, but the next day he comes up on the beach. He swam the whole way. Most men die when they fall in the water. It's so cold you cannot be in it for long. He was in it all night, swimming." Halldor stared at a spot over her shoulder, and his unfocused blue eyes closely resembled Kristjan in a way that the rest of his normally animated face never had.

"Is that why he doesn't talk?" Miranda tried to imagine splashing into the icy seas in winter, the heavy clothes taking on water and sucking her down. She rubbed her fingers against her jeans to dispel the image.

"Some. Also, he has a secret, but I cannot tell of that. It's ill luck to share."

Halldor took a sip of the hot coffee. Miranda had a sudden urge to know this secret, even though sharing such a thing would make them confederates of a sort. The secret drew her like a pearl amongst the rocks.

"Tell me the secret and I'll tell you one of mine."

"Is yours an interesting secret?" He smiled and for a moment she feared he would dangle this bit of knowledge before her without letting her have it.

"Definitely." She wasn't convinced her story would be of interest to him, but she wanted this secret now and would do what was required to get it.

"The story brings ill luck," he said, setting down his cup with a steady, practiced hand. "Less so to us than the man that lived it, but its dark effects may still touch you."

Now Miranda was more determined than ever to hear this tale. Even if it was just a piece of nautical puffery he marched out before naïve tourists.

"Years before my brother was swept off the boat, he was working on another ship. They were fishing in the winter. That's when the fishing is best. So he's pulling up the nets and they feel so heavy. The men wonder if they caught a big seal, but what they find in the net is more like a big serpent. He said it was black like lava rock. The way it shined." Halldor looked up, as though seeing the creature in his mind. "It was tangled in the nets, and as it battled, it was dying. They could not cut the net. If they cut the net, they would go home with nothing. My brother, he helped pull it on the boat. Some of it was still in the water, but the head and front was on the boat. It had a head like a horse's and big fins like a fish, and its mouth was filled with sharp teeth. He said the tail in the ocean splashed the water everywhere as it died. The whole boat shook when the tail hit it. The men on the boat, they cut it up and pulled it out of the net and threw the pieces back into the ocean. They feared what might happen if they had killed a rare beast. One of the men said it was a bad sign."

"What was it?"

"He never knew. Years later when he fell into the sea, people talked. Said it was unnatural to return from those waters." Halldor looked at her with a hint of a grimace turning down the corner of his mouth. Miranda wanted to add these stories to a ball of thread; one for Justin, one for Peter, one each for the Magnusson brothers. Maybe then she could see a way they fit together. As it was, these two stories about Kristjan dropped unfinished into her lap. She could not see where the threads ended or began. She looked at Halldor, searching his face for any involuntary twitch of muscle that might betray a lie. His smile this time was uneasy, settling on the mouth only. That was how one could spot a fake smile, Peter had once told her, by the eyes. Peter said she did it all the time.

Miranda had disliked what she took to be Halldor's familiarity with her. Now she was not so sure that was what his smiles meant.

"Tell me your secret now," he said.

"Later. I'm feeling sick."

"You break your word."

"No, that's not it. I just have to rest. I promise I'll tell you." How could her story compare? Hers was just a petty domestic drama, the most ordinary sort of betrayal.

He encircled her wrist with his rough hand.

"Pledge it."

"I do," she said. As the hum of the engines reverberated through the metal hull, Miranda tried to picture the long, sinuous animal thrashing in the nets, and the faces of the men as their knives pierced its skin.

Above deck, the air was still cold, even in July. Justin monitored several underwater cameras, searching for footage of graceful seals and shimmering fish. On the end of the boat farthest from her, a few crewmen were engaged in loud conversation. Unidentifiable shards of trash floated in the water.

"How about those?" Miranda asked.

"Good, but not the image I need. It has to be something huge, something that will awe and horrify people."

Birds dipped toward the water's surface. The smell of salt

and dead things in the deep came at her again, but did not make her sick. The sun was set in the cloudless sky, spreading a pleasant warmth, rather than the brutal heat she was accustomed to. She looked over his shoulder at the viewscreen. The scent of their fabric softener still lingered on his faded Judas Priest shirt. Justin had been wearing the same shirt when they started dating five years ago. She'd been riveted by his little crusades. She had to get to the bottom of him; to know what lived under the surface. She wanted sieve away all the niceties and be left with a hard, pure essence. Now she wasn't sure that she'd ever really known him. Their life together was just a convenience.

On the screen, the ocean was a dull blue-green. Long skeins of kelp swayed in the current. She could still feel the plastic thread sliding across her fingertips, the periodic hard lump where two strands had to be knotted together.

"What do you know about that Kristjan guy?" she asked once she was sure the Magnusson brothers were not around.

"The captain told me he was in some kind of accident. He was dead for a while, I guess. Probably has brain damage or something."

"Did he really tell you that?"

"I can't remember. Why?" Justin twirled a few strands of her hair around his fingers as he talked.

"Oh, no reason. I just wondered." The sea birds screeched and dove. The lapping of the wavelets against the hull echoed, a sound Miranda could feel down to her feet.

"Isn't it amazing?"

"Who?"

"No, I meant out there," Justin turned Miranda toward the ocean.

She squinted, letting the subtle greys and blacks and blues dissolve into masses of light and darkness. If she looked hard enough, she could almost see the grain of the sea flowing against the sky, the warp and weft that bound light to dark. Almost.

"The whole island of Iceland is being pulled in two by tectonic plates. There are even volcanoes under the glacier that erupt and melt the ice. Then boiling water pours out, sweeping sheep and whole villages out to sea."

"How do they know when it's happening?"

"I guess they don't."

"Nature's secret," Miranda said. Chains clinked in time to the boat's choppy rhythm. The crewmen laughed at a joke. Justin returned to his video monitor.

"I'm glad you came," he said, his eyes fixed on the screen.

"Are you?"

"Of course."

The water rippled. Miranda strained to see if a huge, ancient head would rise out of the water. In the tapestry the muscular coils of Tiamat's body strained against the water, gigantic and unfathomably powerful. Nothing came of the ripple. She wanted to tell Justin about the sea serpent, but it seemed wrong. That was not her tale.

Miranda and Peter worked together at the art supply store. He was twenty-three and said that he was divorced. She thought this was just bullshit. They talked at work sometimes. He showed her the comic strips he drew. Most of them hinged upon lame sci-fi jokes. One night she found him sitting alone in the bar near her house. It was a place she stopped in to have a few drinks on her way home. They talked about the music on the jukebox. It was David Bowie. Peter said he was supposed to meet a girl there—a girl he met online—but she hadn't come. Miranda bought him a beer. She had been prepared to sit alone all night, but having company was better. Her usual routine was to have two drinks and head home while a light buzz floated in her head. This night she felt that floating sensation could very well carry her away to a place that, while perhaps not new, would at least be better.

"Would you like to come over? It looks like you've had a lot. We could watch a movie while you sober up. I don't want you to drive home," Peter had said.

It had been a humid night in early May. The temperature

was already sweltering, even at night. The bar's air conditioning was not up to full blast, and their drinks sweated puddles that soaked through the square paper napkins. Outside the night insects competed with the distant hum of traffic. A dumpster odor mingled with jasmine, the sickening and the sweet. As they walked to Peter's Honda, one yellowing streetlamp flickered and died.

"It's a little messy right now." He let her in. It was dark and hot and also smelled trashy, undercut with an odor of spray paint and pot smoke. She sat on the futon while he groped at a lamp, which did little to dispel the darkness once it was switched on. By the blue glow of the TV, Peter loaded a DVD into the player without asking Miranda what she wanted to see. It was a Star Wars cartoon. While it played, Peter got Miranda a glass of water with lots of ice and opened the sliding door to let in a nonexistent breeze. He said something about the air conditioning when he handed her the glass, but she couldn't hear it over the blaster-gun noises.

Flickering bands of color flashed off his glasses and the glass face of his oversized wristwatch. He sat right next to her. Miranda imagined Justin would be sleeping. She wondered if it was also night in Iceland and if Justin would be sitting up in his bed with a lukewarm can of Coke in his hand. Then she pressed her leg experimentally against Peter's, to see if he would move away. He didn't. He pressed back. Her leg began to tingle with impending numbness. Miranda wanted to shift and make herself more comfortable, but did not want to break this bond, one person touching another. She turned toward him. One spot on his neck was red with razor burn. She put her fingertip on it. His skin was slick with sweat and hotter than the night.

It began as curiosity, but soon her hand was sliding down the collar of his shirt, her own dress sliding up against her sweating legs as he pushed her back against the aluminum bars of the futon and the need to know where this could take her seized her. She could not turn back.

"We shouldn't," he said, pulling his hand away from her thigh.

She had to know what would come next. He bit his bottom lip so hard she expected blood. Crickets and other dwellers in the dirt screeched a chorus of white noise. In silence, he stripped his clothes off. Her skin and his, where it met, alternated hot and cold as the air turned water from their bodies into vapor.

Halldor persuaded Justin to take some time away so that they could break out the bottle of Jack Daniels Miranda brought from the States. They met up in the utilitarian mess room. Kristjan did not join them. Halldor made some meaty stuff in the microwave, along with some runny instant mashed potatoes. Miranda put a spoonful of the soupy potatoes on her plate.

Justin touched her leg under the table. Skin peeled off her fingertips and she wondered if this was some sort if callus-shedding process or a sign of scurvy.

"How is the video?" Halldor asked.

"Okay, I guess. I wish I could get some footage of a really polluted area. Something powerful like that would change people."

Halldor took a long sip from his steel mug of Jack. He looked directly at Miranda.

"Is this to go with the tapestry?"

"I hadn't thought about that," Justin said.

Miranda pushed her potatoes into a mound on one side of her plate. They resembled a small island there. The tapestry was too personal to be used that way. Halldor smirked, as if he knew just how unthinkable his suggestion was.

"Yeah. It's an idea," she said to shut them up.

"You know, I'm thinking about staying longer. At least until the project is finished. Where's a good place we can stay?"

"You and her?" Halldor speared more dark meaty stuff, which was oily and smelled of iron. The scents of rust, booze and unwashed hair made Miranda lightheaded.

"Well, yeah, who else?" Justin squeezed her limp hand under the table.

"I know some people. I might be able to help."

"Maybe Justin would like to hear that story you told me today," Miranda said.

"What story?"

"You might be thinking of something else," Halldor said. He stuffed more meat into his mouth and chewed slowly.

They ate the rest of their dinner in silence.

"I really need to get back to work," Justin said. He kissed Miranda on the top of her head on his way out.

"So, why wouldn't you tell him the story?" she asked once Justin had gone.

"It wasn't for him to know about."

"Or you lied to me."

"You still kept your secret." Halldor pushed his plate aside and reached for the bottle of Jack.

"I don't really have anything worth telling."

"Then tell me about your tapestry. What will it show?" He leaned forward and put his hand palm-up on the table, as if waiting for her to deposit something there.

"That's not much of a secret. It's a Babylonian myth about the beginning of the world, when Marduk kills Tiamat and makes the earth out of her body. See, Tiamat is a dragon. Marduk makes the top half of her into the sky and the bottom half into the sea."

"Why are you making that?" Halldor pulled back. The movement of the boat nearly splashed the liquid out of his cup as he raised it to his lips.

"It's just an interesting story." She didn't want to say that the tapestry was also a net. If she could catch the beginnings of things, maybe she could see the end.

Peter had seen it once. She didn't want to fuck him in the bed she shared with Justin, so they did it on the floor of her study. Afterward, Miranda had gone to get them glasses of water. When she came back, Peter held half the tapestry up, away from himself. His naked body stood outlined by the roiling blues and greens of the ocean. With one hand, he traced the knotted black body of the leviathan as it writhed across

33

the water in its dying agony. He asked her what it showed. Miranda turned the question on him. A test. Would he see it as she had? He said it looked like soft waves breaking under a black sky: a scene of peace and stillness; someone watching the sea from the comfort of a moonlit beach. She told him it was nothing, just some abstract thing she'd been working on.

"That's still just one. I gave you two."

"I don't know what else to tell you."

"There is something," he said.

"I've been fucking this guy I work with. I don't even like him. It's not like he's mad about me either. I thought it might prove something. I don't know what. The worst part about it is that I've never had to remind him to restrain his affection for me. I don't exist when he doesn't see me. That's the secret, people look through me. I just don't exist with them." Miranda digs her spoon into the cold remains of the potatoes. "I'm sorry. None of this has anything to do with you."

"No." Halldor was not smiling.

Miranda left the food on her plate. She felt the yarn slipping through her fingers, slipping away too fast for her to hold on to. She found Justin on the deck, peering through the viewscreen of his handheld digital camera at the horizon.

"Justin, what if something happened?"

"Like what?" He pivoted to take in more of the sea.

"If I slept with someone else."

"Cute. I don't have time to joke right now." He continued to look through his camera at the sea.

"I'm serious," Miranda said. Her heart was pounding. Justin did not anger easily, but she sensed this would do it.

"Yeah, and the punchline is?"

"No, I mean it."

"Get real. I know you're full of shit. Quit joking around." He snapped the camera closed again and turned on her. His face was flushed red, as though with embarrassment. She expected disgust, but his eyes were wide like he'd seen something that scared him. He exhaled hard through his nostrils. Miranda took a step back. The ship bucked, and she reached for the railing. Cold air filled her lungs. Justin's hand hung at his side. He could push her off the boat if he wanted and no one could save her. The icy black water would devour her in one gulp. Justin took a deep breath. Then he smiled mildly, with the eyes and all. "That was a pretty good one. You almost had me."

He laughed then.

"I could really use some sleep. I'm going to bed. Will you be down soon?"

No sounds came out of her mouth. Justin kissed her on the cheek, chuckling to himself as he walked away. He had not believed her. She'd always been so wrong about him.

A cool luminous blue suffused the sky, like light glowing behind a paper screen. The sea was calm. She stood alone against the railing. Unseen things splashed nearby. Miranda followed the cords to the power source and unplugged all Justin's underwater cameras.

Some things can be shared, but others must be kept. Halldor knew it too, and she thought that any minute now she would hear him walking up behind her. It was his story, the one with the long snake creature, its tail still obscured in the sea, that she was meant to hear. She waited on the deck for the serpentine body splitting the sea, the powerful tail lashing through the waves, oil-slick black skin just under the water's surface. She knew it was coming. It had to. Now.

Air and Water

Another Saturday night, and it's raining while she walks to the club. She takes halting steps to keep her heels from filling up with water as she moves over deep puddles forming in the low spots. The speakers inside cranked up high so there's a harsh edge to the bass like something rattling itself loose. The girl behind the bar knows what she wants and mixes it in a clear plastic cup. The fog machine sputters on, flooding the room with the sweet, oily scent of artificial smoke.

Alchemy is the name of this temple of images. Here a towering wall of video flashes glamorous vamps and alien androgynes over the heads of the crowd; the black cupid's bow of Louise Brooks' lips, the arch of David Bowie's eyebrow, the Art Deco planes of Fritz Lang's subversive female android. The demigods of the modern world, as glimpsed through shattered glass. She comes because she wants to believe in magic. Not the bunny-out-of-a-hat kind; the Alistair Crowley kind. This is a ritual.

Under the roulette of images people dance alone, absorbed in their own private spheres. She knows them; the men all too extrinsic, the women too familiar. An antithesis is needed. A perfect chimera that fits into her, anima to animus, puzzle pieces complete.

The mirrorball shatters blue lights into glittering flurries sweeping over a person standing by the wall. She can't tell whether it's a man or a woman. Fragments of light illuminate the face of the figure with a distant, stellar glow, and she thinks this is the one she's been searching for, the half-formed expectation that propels her out to the bars on weekends. Sharp cheekbones and a mouth that's ripe-plum dark and soft. A feminine torrent of black hair. Sharp masculine hips held tight in leather pants. Her lovely chimera, a siren made of the dark air and the glimmering lights of this place. A sense of destiny washes over her like an undertow, pulling her inexorably to her perfect other. If she were to reach out now, she could almost pluck the string of fate pulling them together like the string of a harp and hear the clear note vibrating the air. She drinks to keep her hand from shaking.

Every bleached Sunday morning she goes home alone. But this will be different. This is the one who will fit into her like liquid in a glass. And she doesn't care who this person is. A deep breath inflates her lungs and she holds it in.

Everything stops.

The roof leaks, and the rhythm of the rain falling fills the space in her head. She thinks of the surface of water— how, on a microscopic level, there's no real distinction between where water ends and air begins, and surface tension is an illusion.

The figure seems to be looking at her, and she's pressing back against the bar, its glass surface almost biting into her skin. She's waiting for the figure to come to her and reach out its slender arms, until their surfaces will also mingle, atoms mixing in the no-space between them.

The music crashes in again and the figure walks past her to a group of chattering friends. She can see now the long, smooth neck, the suggestion of breasts as the figure—clearly now a girl—embraces a boy. The boy kisses the girl on the cheek and slips his hand around her waist.

The one she's been seeking still eludes her, and as she watches the boy touch the girl's hair she knows there's no second half to her out there, waiting for her as she's imagined for so long. What she wants can't be given skin, bones, breath. Outside of this room, the images that flicker across the screens die like soap bubbles bursting.

She walks back to the front of the club. Rain comes down in sheets, cascading over the heavy glass panes, the edges clouded by the heat of the air colliding with the cool rain outside. And even if there's nothing really keeping the air and the water separate, there's no way to make the rain fall back into the sky once it's come down.

The drink spills over the empty bottles in the trash, ice clattering on glass. She wipes the condensation from her hand and walks out the front door.

The Worm Vine

Two weeks ago, Diana came home from her job at the phone company and told Paul that she was tired. She thought she'd go to bed for the rest of her life. They moved in a month ago, and though the kitchen wasn't completely organized, Paul managed to cook a frozen pizza and bring her a slice on a paper plate. And when she said she was serious, Paul laughed at her and pulled the sheets up around her neck, patting her arm.

When Diana's boss began calling, she unplugged the phone. Paul told her supervisor that Diana was having some personal problems. They could be sympathetic to that. She hadn't taken more than three days off in two years. They would let her take the days she'd already missed out of her vacation time. But once her time was up, she needed to be back in that office or they would find someone else.

"So you have until Monday." Paul said over the running water in the bathroom. "Did you hear me?" He leaned into the bedroom.

"Yes." She fluffed the head-sized dent out of her pillow.

"So you're going back to work on Monday?" Wisps of steam slithered out of the bathroom.

"I don't know." Leaning back against the headboard, she crossed her arms.

"This is serious. You're going to get fired." At the last word, his voice rose in pitch, an almost girly note of anxiety.

Diana took a book off her nightstand and opened it. It was a book on orchid growing that her neighbor had loaned her. Paul stepped into the shower.

"You're being ridiculous. Diana. Just tell me what's going on." His voice echoed off the bathroom tiles. With the water running, he couldn't have heard anything she said. Last night, she'd made some effort at explaining her exhaustion to him, and he'd told her she really had no reason to feel stressed, that her job couldn't possibly be that exhausting.

She let the book fall closed on the pillow beside her. Burrowing down under the covers, she closed her eyes and waited for the falling sensation of sleep. The shower sounded like rain washing the world clean. She imagined the rain trickling down through layers of soil and rocks to silent cool underground streams.

"Don't pretend that you're sleeping."

"I'm tired."

"We all get tired. We need to have the rent money by next week."

"I'm still getting paid."

"You aren't listening. I want you tell me you're going to be back at work on Monday." He sat on the bed, his weight pulling her unbidden toward him as the mattress sunk.

"I'll see how I feel."

"Come on." He left the wet towel on the bed as he dressed for work. Khaki pants, pleated. She hated pleated pants. They made him look so old.

"I'm just so exhausted. Maybe I'm sick."

"You're not sick. You need to move around. Sleeping too much, that's what's making you so tired."

She knew that wasn't it. Diana pulled the covers up over her ears, but still heard Paul slamming the front door and the metallic roar of his car starting.

She awoke again to the chime of the doorbell. Her eyes stung with the effort of keeping them open. Grabbing her ratty bathrobe, she went down the stairs to the front door and peered out the tiny glass lens. The sunlight hitting her brain was like a powerful flashlight shined directly into her eye. Her neighbor, Ellis, was holding a tan plastic grocery bag. She waited for him to go away. He knocked again, louder.

Diana opened the door.

"Come on in," she said, shielding her face with her hand.

"Thanks. Paul said you've been sick. I brought you some muffins." He set the bag down on the kitchen counter next to a cardboard box marked *Cooking Utensils 2* in black marker.

When Paul and Diana moved in, they sent the neighbors invitations to a housewarming party. It was Paul's idea. Diana didn't want strange people in her house, but he said it was *strategically advantageous* for them to forge relationships in the neighborhood. Paul had started talking that way when the bank promoted him, as if by absorbing corporate bullshitese he would convince himself that he really belonged there. Ellis was the only person who showed up to the party. He was a tree surgeon. He had some suggestions for the tree in their yard. Afterward, Diana had waved Ellis' business card under Paul's nose chanting *strategically advantageous, strategically advantageous*, until she eked a laugh out of him.

Ellis's back yard was visible from the bedroom window upstairs. Diana often watched him tending his garden or leaving cat food in empty plastic deli containers for the neighborhood strays. His yard was stuffed with luscious green plants, unlike the patches of dirt breaking through the weedy grass on her side of the fence. Diana thought his yard was full of strange violet butterflies until she came close enough to see that they were flowers, poised on an impossibly thin stalk rising from the orchids he grew. He said he took dying plants from the dumpsters behind Home Depot and coaxed them back to life.

Ellis sat down at the kitchen table and scratched the dark scruff on his face as he looked at the room. His short brown hair was damp and carried the crisp scent of chlorinated pool water.

"You all haven't finished unpacking?"

"No. I'm taking some time off." Diana filled a saucepan with water and put it on the stove. A stack of paint chips rested on the counter next to Diana's unopened mail. She had mulled over the colors, labeling the backs of the chips with the rooms she wanted to paint. The square of teal blue she'd wanted for her bathroom now seemed dull, water standing in a puddle. She swept the chips into the garbage.

"From work?"

"From life." She said it with a shrug. The gas hissed as the blue flame spit out of the burner.

"Ah." A thin line of black marked Ellis's nails as he drummed them on the table. Dirt, trapped under his nails. "So, those orchids we picked up seem to be doing well." He retrieved the bag containing the muffins and peeled away the sealing tape.

Diana squirted dish soap on a sponge and washed the two mugs in the sink.

It had been three weeks since Ellis had taken her on his orchid collecting expedition. They walked to where the woods were being cleared for a new housing development. Ellis explained to her how it was likely illegal for them to take the plants, but otherwise, they would be mulched along with the trees when the construction crew returned tomorrow. He told her how orchid seeds are blown to Florida from the Caribbean by hurricanes; how one orchid makes millions of seeds from one flower, though only one or two will land in a place with the right fungus to make the seed grow. The spider orchid had brown flowers with petals like long, ragged ribbons. A bloom of the clamshell orchid had a red, pouting lip with thin chartreuse petals that hung down like a squid's tentacles. The scent of pine sap and freshly turned soil and the dark green of rotting leaves penetrated Diana's nose as Ellis talked. They picked through the hacked-up limbs and flaky trunks; no birds calling.

"When it gets cooler, I might move them into the porch." Ellis peeled the paper off a muffin.

When they returned to Diana's house, Ellis showed her how to attach the orchid to a slab of wood. He attached plastic-coated wire to the slab and looped it over a tree branch. She said it looked like it was on a raft, floating in the air on this little wooden raft. It would get the rain and air it needed there, he said. Orchids lived off of rain and air. In the wild, one plant could live for decades, very slowly sending out roots that crept up, clinging firmly to the bark of a tree as it reached for the light. She thought this would be a very exhausting way to live, just crawling up for years and years, never actually getting anywhere.

"How's that one I gave you?"

"Oh," Diana stretched on the tips of her toes so she could see the tree in her yard. The mass of brownish green wormy roots swayed on its little raft. "It looks pretty good. I haven't been watering it since it's been raining lately." She set out the two cups, dropped a tea bag into each and poured in the boiling water; a familiar aroma of tannin rising from the cups. Diana took Ellis a cup, but left hers on the counter. She preferred to wait until the tea was dark brown like river water.

"So, when do you go back to work?" Ellis dropped muffin crumbs on the table as he tore pieces off.

"I'm not sure. I really don't want to."

"Seriously."

"I don't know." She sighed and walked back to the counter, lifting the cup of tea and sniffing it. "Paul is all pissed off."

"Well, what did you tell him?"

"Same thing I just said. I'm not going back to work. I can't go out there."

"Outside?" Ellis wiped muffin crumbs from his mouth with the back of his huge hand.

"Outside or anywhere. Anything can happen to you out there." Diana gestured toward the door, the robe's belt slackening as she moved. She tightened it, though she was wearing a set of black pajamas covered in little blue birds.

"That's usually the idea."

"I can't keep up." She took her cup of tea and sat at the table. Ellis held out a muffin, and she set it next to her cup. If she told Ellis, it would sound just as petty as Paul made her sound.

"Why? Are you afraid something will happen to you?"

"I don't know." She was getting tired of repeating this phrase.

When they were gathering the orchids, Ellis showed her what to look for. Some species grew thick, waxy leaves in which they stored water; some grew thick jointed stalks like deranged green fingers; some were nothing more than a knot of ropy roots tangled into bark. The worm-vine was a name for a kind of vanilla that grew only on the west coast of the state. It had no leaves, just branching masses of roots that turned orange when the sunlight hit them. When she asked if they were hurting the tree, he laughed and said no, they only use the outer bark to anchor themselves. A white layer covering the roots took in water and air. Damp October air carried the mingled scents of the disturbed earth and the gasoline the saurian machines ran on. She gave up counting the felled trees. Diana kept herself from asking how long it may have taken for this tract of forest to grow. Everywhere she looked, she saw nothing but pointless struggle.

"Well, whatever you think might come about is probably a hundred times worse than reality. Trust me."

"Oh yeah?" Maybe Ellis could understand. She wasn't the victim of some hormonal fluctuation, as Paul said.

"Yeah. I've been through really rough times myself and, personally, I've seen how bad shit really gets." Ellis took a sip of the tea and grimaced.

"What's that supposed to mean?" She knew nothing about this man. He raised plants, fed stray cats, worked outside. He liked some of the same bands Paul used to listen to: Black Flag, Exploited, The Damned. He knew how to make things grow. He'd listened to her tedious work stories and even laughed a few times.

"Can I have some sugar?"

"We don't have any right now." She was alone with him in the house and she didn't even know his last name. It wasn't on his mailbox.

"Okay."

"What are you talking about?"

"Well, I used to be really into drugs." Ellis used his finger to scoop the wet tea bag out of the cup. He set it among a pile of crumbs on the muffin wrapper. "For a while there I was using dope pretty regularly. I started out working in this restaurant. Everyone there was pretty fucked up most of the time. One of the waitresses used to think it was funny to give me speed and tell me it was Valium." His tanned arms revealed a lighter shade of skin as he moved his arm, the place on his bicep where his shirt protected him from the sun.

"When was this?"

"I was going to college. It was my first time away from home, and man, I thought it was time to really cut loose and party. Long story short, this guy I worked with hooked me up with some friends he partied with. They had insane parties. Crazy girls, coke."

"And this is when you?" Diana let her voice trail off. She wasn't sure what post-junkie etiquette was. It might be improper to say *addict*.

"Oh yeah, it was great. It made everything else look so far away. You couldn't give a shit about anything except how fucking great it felt. So you let everything slide."

Diana had never considered that her new neighbor might have something like this in his past. It was absurd, living next to an after-school-special. She imagined a younger Ellis with the greasy, furtive look they gave addicts on crime shows. Beat-up dirty sneakers; a heather grey t-shirt ringed with blackened sweat at the collar, radiating from the armpits; a black hoodie, unzipped. She imagined sleepless nights on mattresses soaked with desperation and fingernails torn bloody.

"After I stopped going to classes, I got bounced out of my dorm, so it was crashing with friends all the time. Then I started having fewer and fewer friends I could call on. I didn't have anything to sell anymore. I hung out in the library a lot because I could sleep there." He paused and looked down into the cup.

"Then?"

"People get weird about it. I understand, I guess, but it's my honest experience."

"What is?"

"Well, I did get saved eventually." Ellis looked away. And Diana was sure he was seeing it too: the gaps in the windows, the line of ants marching out to eat a dead bird in the yard, the useless grass growing just to get crushed under their feet.

"By who?"

"Jesus Christ."

Diana pushed away an image of sweaty addict Ellis being approached in the library by the dude who was on all the candles in the Latino groceries. She pictured Jesus picking Ellis up of the floor, dusting him off and putting a pruning saw in his hand; pushing him out the door to live on as her next door neighbor. There was a divinely ordained mission: prune thy trees. She waited for a punchline. Ellis just looked into her eyes like he was waiting for her to kiss him. The gently pleading look middle school boys used to give her when they wanted to touch her breasts.

"I know it's not really for everyone, but finding religion really helped me. Without the knowledge that my suffering was for a higher purpose, I would never have gotten clean." Ellis stood, went to the sliding glass door that led outside and parted the blinds. The sharp fall sunlight slid over his damp hair, igniting strands of ruddy brown. Diana almost laughed. She was wrong. He wasn't looking at what she saw at all.

"Your suffering was for a higher purpose?" She tried not to let a bitchy tone slice through her words, but it came out regardless.

"Yes. It was. It might even help you to come with me sometime."

Diana could not picture anything emptier than a pack of old rituals to toss into the void.

No pain served a higher purpose. Pain perpetuated itself, and once touched, it would come back again and again. Life shifted up and down, producing nothing in the end but suffering and decay. It might start as miles of dead forest, the struggle and crush of life pushing, grinding to go on and on and on; the endless turn of death and decay and then life again, over and over. She'd had to witness that on her own. Even the orchids growing—a scrap of existence squeezed out of entropy—now appeared alien and revolting on with their wormy roots clutching the rotting wooden mounts.

"How do you know that?"

"I have faith."

"Well, that must be nice, but I don't see a purpose in anything that happens on this planet." Diana went back to the sink and dumped out her cup. The dark tea disappeared down the drain, leaving no trace on the steel surface.

"How can you say that?"

"Can't you see it? What do we do that really matters? What's the fucking point in trying?" Her voice rose.

"So your answer is to just stop trying to do anything?" He crossed his arms over his chest. "That's so selfish."

Selfish. That had been the thrust of an argument she had with Paul three nights ago. She wasn't thinking about what Paul needed. She had obligations to him. She knew that, but she was tired. She tried to explain how heavy her bones had gotten, like the weight of the air had become unbearable. He said she was just lazy. She could not tell him how all she saw on her drive home from work were dead animals; piles of fur crumpled in the dirt. Anything that lived seemed destined to putrefy into mud. Every time she looked out the window, she saw the rotted gaps in the wooden fence, the line in the cinderblock that prophesied a crack, the orange surveying paint that augured more huge piles of forest crushed to make room for another road. She could only say she was tired.

"You don't get it," she said.

"No, you don't. I want to help. Have you considered counseling?" Ellis sat down and grasped her hand. His thick fingers put so much pressure on her that she felt her bones rolling against each other. She felt she'd wandered into a trap.

"How can you possibly?" She wanted to know. There was nothing he could do for her. He'd shown her the dead forest. Ellis had told her about the long life of the orchid; its supreme effort to flower perhaps once in five or ten years, only to have its seeds blown into the ocean, wasted. Wasted. Now that she'd seen the careless squandering of nature, she could not stop. It drew her like the mosquitoes that swarmed around the lightbulb on their porch. She was drained, constricted by a strangling vine she'd been oblivious to until Ellis showed her it was there.

"All I ask is that you keep an open mind," Ellis said.

Diana's hand sweated in his grip. Her dry mouth tasted of unbrushed teeth and the leathery tang of black tea. Her lips moved, but her voice caught in her throat.

"You need perspective. Whatever you're going through right now, it can't be that bad."

"You can't help me," she said. Diana pulled her hand away.

"I can, if you let me. Things may look bad now, but suffering makes the salvation so sweet." He'd seen the dead forest, and he was just as unmoved by it as Paul would have been. There was a manic glint in his eye, as though the idea of pain excited him.

"I think you should go now."

Ellis stepped back as if slapped. He tilted his head and his eyebrows came together in a concerned expression. A look of pity. Diana ran water over her cup in the sink. The door opened and closed, and with it a shift in air pressure let her know she was alone.

Diana made sure the door was locked. On her way up the stairs, she saw a dead fly on the carpet, its stiff legs thrust up in the air like radio towers. From her window, she spied on Ellis as he trimmed dried tendrils from a passionfruit vine that clambered over an arched trellis. His back, straight and stiff as though he knew she was watching, was a plank. Maybe his faith gave him a shield against the decay that surrounded them. A spear of guilt pricked Diana. Ellis didn't set out to pull back the curtain of comfortable illusion she'd lived with. It wasn't his fault he couldn't share this with her.

Paul would come home and fight with her again. And if she spent all day rehearsing what she would say to him, she would still not be able to explain. He'd traded his soul for a pile of self-improvement books that coached him to get that promotion; make himself indispensable; give *outrageous* customer service.

When she and Ellis had been out in the woods together, she'd wondered what it might be like, clinging to life while hanging in the air twenty feet above the ground. The rainstorm could be an answered prayer. Blind years would pass before she felt the sun warming one bent root as it strained toward the treetops. Pretty flowers now mocked her; the waxy upthrust sexes of groping plants hanging from breakable stalks. Everyone was grasping and hoping that they didn't fall. She'd been pulling herself up by her fingertips. It would be so much easier to just let go.

Diana let the aluminum blinds click back into place. She wiped the smudges of dust from her fingers. A clatter of metal as Ellis fired up his lawnmower. In her quiet bedroom, Diana imagined herself sleeping out the erosions that would wear the house down to rounded humps of concrete. The lock on the door was broken, so after she took all of Paul's clothes out of the dresser and piled them neatly in the hallway, she slid the dresser up against the door.

In all likelihood, Paul would find a way to get past her barricade. If not through brute force, then by calling the fire department, or perhaps the police. Diana wondered if he would have her committed. She lay down on the bed, her eyelids burning with weariness after moving the furniture. There was a roll of duct tape in the closet. She would begin taping over the windows after she took a nap.

Diana closed her eyes and waited for sleep to drop her into darkness.

A Floating World

She had never danced. Of course not, she said, she'd been born without feet. He took a sip of his white wine. She recognized the look: a slight affront, perhaps, at her bluntness. It was just another fact. She had red hair, she sunburned easily, and her legs—fully formed above the knee—tapered below it to stumps that would never bear her weight. He joked that it was a good thing he wasn't a foot fetishist and held his breath until her lips curved into a smile. She said she loved that he didn't treat her like she was made of glass. Glass is too transparent, he said, and she was not a woman he could ever look through.

She worked with jellyfish. Special fins had been made for her legs that allowed her to skim through the ocean like a seal. Whenever she put them on she imagined herself as the two-tailed Orisha she had once seen stamped into a silver medallion in a Jamaican shop. As she spooled angel hair onto her fork she described the weightless lives of these creatures: an alien existence, drifting in the warm currents, silently waiting for prey to be swept into their trailing tentacles. Something we land dwellers likely couldn't comprehend.

After dinner they returned to her house and had sex. As he touched her legs—the hands she found not quite as steady as she'd expected a surgeon's to be—she realized he was feeling under the skin, sensing the bone structure, the musculature such as it was over the slender pegs that she'd inherited in lieu of feet. He pressed, leaving a thumbprint where her ankle might have been. Men had avoided touching her there; fearful, perhaps, of causing pain or crushing a delicate bone even though she told them how strong her legs could be in the water as each steady kick propelled her forward. The surgeon didn't need her reassurances. She thought it was as if he knew already that despite her body she was strong and complete and later she would say it was that fearless touch that made her fall in love with him.

We can guess at the rest. Keys exchanged. Drawers in the bedroom given over to the lover's socks and underwear. A small collection of personal items left behind—a bill, a pair of running shoes, a sky-colored button-down shirt—accumulating a shared history. He learned to navigate the kitchen that had been purpose-built to be accessible to her wheelchair. He took her to charity balls where she joked to anyone who asked that a shark had bitten her feet off. On one these nights, drunk on champagne that someone else's compassion had paid for, he said that they might as well get married in the offhanded voice she had come to recognize as his way of shielding himself. She turned away from the beads of rain shimmering on the car window and said she couldn't see a good reason why not. He broke into laughter as the rain pelted out a rhythm on the windshield.

In her lab she observed the jellyfish in their tanks trailing a tattered gown of stinging tentacles through the water. Her hands grasped the wheels of her chair and she rolled to another specimen. A tiny fish floated upside down in the tangle of tentacles.

Passivity is no guarantee of harmlessness.

A grad student asked what she meant. She shrugged him away. With a net, she lifted a jellyfish from the tank. In the air, its body collapsed into a translucent mass. The surgeon wanted to have a seaside wedding. To her, the ceremony was beside the point. She imagined he wanted the setting to be some concession to her—a reminder of the ocean in which her body felt at its most powerful. She had already proven to him in the pool at his gym how with her fins she was faster and more graceful in the water than any other swimmer. Her jellyfish brought her back to the clumsiness of life on land. The grad student hunched over his notes, tapping his pencil against his teeth while the dead fish made its slow inevitable way toward the mouth of the jellyfish to be digested.

It was at another charity ball that the surgeon told her of his plans. An artist had been hired to create an installation depicting domestic violence. The result was a room carpeted with shards of broken mirror in which some android-like female figures posed, headless—menaced from above by black words cut from acrylic and hung on steel cables. Much was made of the very important work of this very important artist, but she found herself with little patience for this type of talk and imagined herself peacefully underwater, moving through that muffled space like a seal. The surgeon interrupted her reverie to steal away a moment with her on the balcony. There he announced the very special gift he was planning to give her. She did not understand at first.

A pair of beaded silk pumps? Was this a joke?

No, he said, a promise. The transplants would come from a donor, but he would make every effort to find someone of similar build so that they would look natural. The work he'd been doing with nerve connections had been very promising. He couldn't yet say if she would have full sensation, but he was sure that with time and therapy she would have a full range of motion.

She shook her head.

He meant walking?

Yes, he said, and more. Walking, running, dancing. Freedom.

And what about the pain?

She knew he would never intentionally hurt her, didn't she? He wouldn't tell her it was going to be easy, but wasn't she willing to take the risk if it meant a new life?

She thought for a few days. Laps in the pool, the water shimmering and breaking ahead of her as she came up to breathe and plunged down again. She swam to the looping doubts in her mind. She had never considered anything like what the surgeon was now offering her. Life was as it always had been for her. Wishing for another way was fruitless. Still her imagination went back and forth, as if two selves beckoned to her from the future. One standing proud in the shoes he had given her; a glance over the shoulder across a room filled with revelers, a wave of red hair, a dare and a slick of crimson lipstick. Another floated solipsistic and complete in the deep blue; her legs more like the tail of a whale than the pale knobby limbs she witnessed when she opened her eyes under the water. She sat at the bottom of the pool and waited, eyes closed as though listening for something only she could hear.

She returned home from the gym that night and told him of her decision. He held her hands and whispered his excitement. They would dance at their wedding. She looked down at her legs and tried to imagine whether there would be a seam where the new feet were stitched on. His hands over hers were warm and solid. She knew he would do his best.

After the operation everything from her hips down ached. The surgeon was at her bedside, explaining that the bruising and swelling would subside. The feet seemed the color and texture of frozen fish. He said that it would take some time for the new blood supply to bring the color back to the skin, but that so far her progress was excellent and the surgical team expected her to make a full recovery. All these medical clichés struck her as meaningless as she looked down upon the alien parts that had been grafted onto her body. Her own skin was puffy and violet-blue where it met the skin of the feet. She dreamed that she would enter the ocean only to find the feet had been carved from stone and they would drag her straight to the bottom. In time the swelling did subside as the surgeon had promised. Each night he tended to her new appendages with the attention of a priest performing a holy rite. Once the stitches were removed he carefully applied ointment to the seam so that the scarring would be minimal.

Therapy was frustrating. Her body had been unaccustomed to the jerking motions of walking. Where her new foot touched the ground the fire of a thousand needles shot up her legs. The weight of her body poised above her feet seemed unbearable. At the end of each session her joints thrummed with pain. The legs that cut so cleanly through the water were limp joints of meat on land, flopping out from under her at surprising times. She survived by closing her eyes and imagining herself a medusa in the floating world, careless and nearly bodiless on the warm current. She learned to take her mind off the pain, but the pain never truly allowed her to leave it behind. It held her as tightly as a net.

With the surgeon's help she acclimatized herself to her new parts: shoes, the clipping of toenails, stepping on wet tiles, hot beach sand underfoot. Throughout the pain pricked at her again and again. The surgeon took her to the best specialists, but they could provide her with no relief. She found herself retreating to what she had begun to think of as her blue world more often to escape. Often the disconnect was so complete that she would come to awareness as though waking from an enchanting dream to find the surgeon had been awaiting a word from her. As their wedding date approached, she used the stress of planning as an excuse to slip away into her world.

The day arrived at last. She wore the shoes he had given her a year earlier. He wanted her to know that he had fulfilled his promise. She found walking in them tricky, even though she had practiced many times before this. The balancing act required to stay upright made her knees ache. Pain licked at her feet like fire. She thought back to night when he had given her the shoes. The artist and his room of glass shards. She felt she was trapped in that room as she stepped toward the door. Her days of circuits in the pool seemed to her an endless loop that some part of herself was now still swimming; like the shark that must swim or die. Those were the last days of her old life. Needles puncturing the feet that were still someone else's feet though nourished by her own blood; nerves screaming into her own nerves. She would be married to the surgeon. He wanted her to dance with him.

He stood awaiting her in the reverent silence she knew well from his somber attentions to her healing scars. Planks of wood had been put down over the sand to help steady her feet. The green salty tang of the ocean rushed into her lungs with each breath. She concentrated on putting one foot in front of the other without crying out as the needles dug further into the tender core of her feet. The roar of the waves sounded louder now to her than the music they had chosen together for her walk. It pounded in her ears like her own blood; like the cracking electrical impulses singing pain through her nerves. She closed her eyes for a momentary glimpse of the deep blue. The last thing she felt was the bouquet slipping from her fingers.

She was aware of voices around her. She moved as if caught in a powerful current, as if being drawn into a riptide. The surgeon called her name and she nearly turned back but she felt now the pull of the ocean drawing her near. She couldn't feel the feet anymore, but a lingering pressure told her she must be walking across the sand into the water. The surgeon screamed her name in panic she'd never heard before and she froze, her muscles clenching in a moment of sympathy for all that was expressed in those syllables. The waves were at her neck now, and she felt as though she was dissolving into them. A thread that was keeping her tethered to the shore tugged at her mind but she could barely remember what it was. A touch? It was soon lost in the blue and she felt herself floating toward the silent bottom of the sea, weightless and without boundary, as if her body had been a heavy dress, as if she had gladly unzipped it and wriggled her way out.

Static

It's Michelle's birthday, and she wants Drew to be her birthday present. And she knows she'll get him tonight because the oracle book told her so. They're in her kitchen, under the one fluorescent light that still works, while somebody—a friend of a friend she hadn't met before tonight—is mopping up spilled Diet Coke with a napkin. The few other people left in her apartment, are too involved in other business to interrupt.

The oracle book is in her bedroom, hidden under her pillow. Before people arrived for the party she'd asked it if Drew would sleep with her tonight. *An open road lies before you*, it said, in the ambivalent language of horoscopes and tarot manuals. She'd tested it once by asking if her name was Michelle. *Rely on your imagination*, it said. Then she asked if she was going to win the lottery, though she'd never bought a ticket and had no plans to. *If you will respect yourself in the morning*. She thought that meant that she would do something embarrassing if she had that much money, like buy a mansion and put inflatable furniture in it.

"Did you know that static is actually radiation from stars?" She shouts, so Drew will hear her over the thudding music.

Drew's got this light green polo shirt on, and the silver spheres of a ball-chain flash against his chest when he leans down to speak. "Like a microwave?"

"Static electricity", she'd read that in *Glamour* or *Jane*— a crush that you enjoy without expecting fulfillment—and she thought that Drew was her inert thrill, a little shock that neither satisfied or hurt. But tonight his white teeth are almost glowing in the dark when he smiles, and he smells like juniper—he's drinking gin and juice—and his arm is resting on the counter so casually it's like he already knows it's going to happen.

"It's like, leftover radiation from the big bang." She traces the outline of the Hammer of Thor tattooed on his bicep.

"So there could be a message from God in there?"

"The gods," she corrects.

"Let's check your TV and see if we get any messages."

She pretends to be too drunk to walk so she can hold on to his arm as they make their way past the late-night loiterers to the living room. Michelle turns it to a dead channel and the screen lights up with snow. Drew sits next to her on the third-hand couch and doesn't resist her hand sliding up his arm.

"I think I see something," she says. His face is so close she can see the few reddish hairs on his neck that he missed when shaving.

She waits for the TV to tell him what she already knows from the oracle book.

A triple-chirp issues from the pocket of his pants. He looks at his phone. The screen says *Kerry*, the name of his on again-off again girlfriend. Michelle thought they were supposed to be off now.

"I'd better take this," he says, and walks out the sliding glass door to the balcony. Drew lifts the phone to his ear.

Michelle goes past a besotted couple making out in the hallway to her room, closes the door and reaches for the book under her black pillowcase. Out in the living room a reveler is laughing a laugh she doesn't recognize. Drew's silhouette paces outside her window, a stretched shadow on the blinds.

"Do I even have a chance with him?" Her breath has alchemized the drink to a sour brew. She lets her fingers slide over the pages, pulling the book open when it feels right.

If it's meant to be, it will just happen, printed in curving black letters on the eggshell page. Outside, Drew is laughing at something his girlfriend just said.

Meditate on it tonight, the book suggests. Like she hasn't been watching Drew over the shoulders of her friends all night, trying to interpret how close he stands, every nuance of his posture.

"I don't know. Maybe later. . ." Drew says. He must be trying to get Kerry off the phone. She checks her semi-smeared mascara in the mirror.

Michelle tosses the book onto her bed and it falls open to *You need to tone it down.* Just beyond her bedroom door, voices are asking where she is. The last partiers prepare to leave. Michelle moves closer to the window so she can hear Drew over the others.

"Tell you about it tomorrow," Drew says. "I'm getting pretty tired. Besides..."

"Birthday girl," someone calls.

Michelle holds the book between her palms. She asks again, turning the pages until she sees the right answer. *You will succeed according to your wish.*

Our Lady of Wormwood

I met Ian at the end of the world.

No, my story doesn't start there. It starts with a death. My father moved us to America when I was too young to remember. Once he had been an artist working in religious icons; gilded and rarefied images of saints. He used his artistic talents to create different sorts of icons when we landed in New York; where once his brush had stroked gold into the halo around Saint Artemius of Antioch, he now illustrated the hypnotic chrome glow of the new Chevrolet Impala. We were just two. It was one of his business partners that got me my first modeling job; a toothpaste ad. In our apartment, one remaining icon that he'd been able to bring with him to the states hung in his study. For a long time, I thought this gentle, beautiful golden woman was my mother. Even after I learned the portrait was of Saint Catherine, I still conjured her image in my mind on the rare occasions my father spoke of my mother. She was always a mystery wrapped in halos. I grew up, started making some money, moved out. When he died, I found letters he'd written to her. I couldn't read Cyrillic, but I did know enough recognize the name *Anna*. I'd always assumed he didn't miss her like I did. The letters filled a wine crate. These letters and the icon sat in my closet, a void written out in a language I couldn't read; reminders that I'd never really known my father either.

I started getting better contracts, had my picture taken a lot, partied hard to keep myself from dwelling on that box of mystery.

Waking up in my loft apartment one morning in February, the guitarist for some hot new band sprawled across my bed; spilled bottles of vodka leaving clear dried syrup on the hardwood floor, the TV showed me something I could not forget—a documentary about Chernobyl. On the screen glowed a painted icon of Our Lady of Chernobyl, her golden halo intersecting a radiation symbol. And I remembered a story my father had once told me, about an icon he had hidden in his apartment years ago, when we lived near the nuclear plant there. I tried to picture it often, something beautiful and gold, touched with a mystery that I could not comprehend. An image crafted by the hand of the man I'd called father. And maybe if I could find it, I could start to understand a bit more who my father had been.

Once I had delusions that I could peer into the mysteries of the world, slice them open with a flashlight. I would dig out the truth, no matter how deep it was buried. I spent hours staring at that Saint Catherine, trying to see exactly how each stroke of paint went on. My private attempts to recreate the painting were embarrassingly inadequate. I wanted to create pictures that glowed with an inner mystique, but I ended up just another pretty thing. Instead of making the image, I became the image. Art school was a struggle that was much easier to give up once I started making a career out of modeling. That February morning, I kicked out the guitarist and tracked down Ian Rufus. He agreed to meet me in Chernobyl.

We met at a small café. I wore dark sunglasses and a black knit hat, hoping no one would recognize me. Not that Glamourlash or Flawless Visage were things that anyone around would have given a shit about. Finally, I took my glasses off, thinking about that asshole actor I went out with who insisted on wearing his sunglasses inside a club all night. The guy a few tables away kept looking at me. His hair was shaved off, a kind of colorless stubble delineating a receding hairline. He was a little chubby, wearing oval glasses with thin silver frames, dressed in a black leather biker jacket and smoking while he read *Foucault's Pendulum*. Finally, he got up and walked over to my table.

"I'm sorry, are you Maryska?" He had an English accent.

"Yes."

"I'm Ian. How do you do?" He shook my hand and sat down. "I've arranged for a guide to take us into the zone. He should be here momentarily."

"Why do you want to go, then?" he asked after a moment.

"I need to find something."

"So what do you do?"

"I do some modeling," I said.

"Really? Must be profitable."

"Yeah, well, I'm nearing the end of my run, I'm sure."

"Oh, come on, you look young."

"I'm only twenty-one, but it's getting pretty tiring."

"So what are you going to do next?"

"What do you mean?"

"After you're done modeling." He took a cigarette out of his pocket and lit it, the blue plume rising over his head as he exhaled. I put my hand out and he gave me one, holding the flame of his lighter to the tip after I placed it between my lips.

"I haven't really thought about it," I said. "How about reporting? What's that like?"

"It's interesting. I write about unexplained phenomena, strange occurrences, and pretty much anything else that people think is weird. I was just finishing up a story about feral children." He carefully tapped his ashes into a tin ashtray.

"What?"

"You know, children who are raised by animals. Since the Soviet Union collapsed, there's been more unemployment and alcoholism. Sometimes the young ones are left alone or wander off and end up with the packs of wild dogs. They're taken in by the animals." He took off his glasses and rubbed at his eyes.

"I thought that kind of stuff was just a myth."

"There are stranger things."

"And this is what you write about?"

"It's a niche market, certainly."

"So, have you ever seen anything that proves it?"

"Proves what?"

"Unexplained phenomena," I said.

"I'll say that I don't believe these things are random or made up. There's connectivity to the universe that we can't perceive. If we could see everything that is true we'd lose our minds. Our inability to set all this in order is all that keeps us sane."

The morning sun illuminated eddies of smoke swirling around the room. I felt like I wanted to like him. There was a softness around him that seemed comforting. He wasn't the kind of guy I would have normally had any interest in. Maybe that was it. His ordinariness was new to me.

"What about you? Why would a beautiful girl like you come here?"

"I was born there, in Pripyat. I don't remember any of it. We, my father and I, left when I was only three. My mother had been a technician at the plant. Died a few years after I was born." The ceiling had a film of age over the white paint. In one corner the paint bubbled, cracks radiating out of it, as though something was slowly poking its way down from the floor above. "He died two years ago. He never would have wanted me to come here."

"Christ. I'm sorry. Here," he said, pulling a tissue out of his jacket and handing it to me. I took the limp white square from him, but I wasn't crying. I balled up the tissue in my fist and held it there. All the tears were long gone.

"That's okay," I said. "It's fine, really. I mean, I have everything you could ever want. I couldn't have that if I'd been here." I wondered if he thought that made me some sort of an orphan. I guess that's what I was, but I'd never really thought of it that way until I had to explain it to him.

"Aren't you worried about going into the contaminated zone?"

"Not really. Are you?"

The question seemed to startle him. "Bad things could happen to you. This isn't a bloody vacation spot. You're just a kid."

"And what about you?"

"I've been around. I'll make sure you're okay."

A thin man in a bright red and black Motocross jacket came in and looked around the room. A small scar arced over his left eyebrow. His face was shadowed by dark stubble, his eyes icily blue. One his right hand, a crude tattoo of a naked woman decapitated by his sleeve marked his skin. The left hand also had a band of darkness around his middle finger, though it had faded into a mere inkblot. He had a dampness to his shirt, as if he'd slept and sweated and been rained on in the same clothes for a week. I wondered if this man, or another like him, would have been part of my life had things been different. Perhaps, if I had stayed here, I would have run off with a man like this and lived long enough to regret it. He looked around the room and walked toward my table.

"Are you Ian Rufus?" he asked.

"Yes," Ian said.

"I am Vanko Kvitkin. You wanted a guide. I will take you." He pulled out a cigarette and lit it, dragging a third chair to our table.

"As per our arrangement," Ian said. He reached into his jacket and pulled out a wad of money held together with a beige rubber band. It thumped down onto the table. Vanko grabbed it and stuffed it into his jacket, looking over his shoulder as he did.

"Have care, friend," he said. "You're going to get robbed if you act like this." He crushed out his cigarette on the saucer that came with my tea.

The town was still wreathed in the colorlessness of early spring. Outside, the road was wet with melted snow, the scrawny trees still slumbering, not a hint of green to be seen. We all piled into Vanko's car and set out for the contaminated zone.

"You must have hundreds of stories," I said to Ian.

"All right. A friend of mine was walking his dog in the woods near his house. This was out in the country and the path was narrow. The dog bolted off the path toward the trees," He rolled down the car window to let some of the smoke out. "Where was I? Yes, my friend thinks his dog must be after a

67

hedgehog or mouse, so he follows the dog into the woods to see what he's caught. He finds the dog a little ways off the path barking at what he described as a tall man dressed all in black. He thought it a bit strange to see someone alone, off the path. He apologized profusely, and dragged the dog away. It wasn't until after he got home that he recalled that the man seemed to have no face. He wasn't just dressed in black, he was all of darkness. He described it as being like a great hole punched in the world, where nothingness leaked through."

"So, did he ever see it again?"

"Not that he's told me."

"What do you think it was?" I put my hand on the back of the seat. The cracked white vinyl upholstery of the car felt like eggshells.

"I don't know. Possibly it was a glimpse into another reality. There's more than one, you know. There are places where you can cross from one to another."

"And you? Have you done this?"

Vanko snorted. Ian looked at Vanko, and he forced a cough to cover his reaction.

"Not yet," he said. As the car bumped over the road into a dead town, I looked out to the snowy fields and wondered where the flowers would burst out in the spring. I tried to imagine my father here as a boy. He had grown up in another town, but I tried to picture a young boy with his serious eyes wading through knee-high poppies in the fields. The summer winds would have ruffled wheat-colored hair out of his eyes as he turned to listen to the song of a turtle dove. Maybe he would be noticing the way the sun blazes through the red petals of the poppy, turning the black interior golden-plum. His little fingers would close around one fuzzy green stem and with a twist and upwelling of bitter milk, he would take the poppy home so he could capture its flaming petals on paper. I closed my eyes. A nice picture, even if I couldn't quite believe it happened that way. It was at least something to plug into the gaps.

We were stopped on our way into the zone. Two soldiers with machine guns flagged us down, both of them peering into the car sullenly, holding their guns as if they were prosthetic hands. One of them talked to Vanko in Russian. He seemed to reassure them, then he turned to us and shrugged, though in a rehearsed way, as though he expected this and wanted to use this situation.

"There is problem," he sighed, without much conviction. "We need permits to go in. But he says maybe he will pretend he never saw us, for a price."

The young soldier nodded at his companion, his cold stare never leaving me. He was beautiful in the brutal way soldiers are. I reached into my coat, where I'd hidden two parcels of money and handed one up to Vanko. Ian leaned forward and pulled some cash out of his back pocket. Vanko took both bundles and handed them out the window. The soldier lit a cigarette and tossed the money to his companion to be counted. They both nodded and stepped away from the car.

I sat in the back seat of Vanko's car and smoked as we approached the contaminated zone. The window had a hairline crack in it, just deep enough to distort the glass. We passed a troop of prehistorically shaggy horses running through the slushy dead grass. Here, where men had left them behind, they had reverted to an earlier form, it seemed. The poisonous earth seemed to have no effect of the wild things, though it did dawn on me that the entire herd could be riddled with cancer. Steam threaded its way into the air from their nostrils.

"Look at that," Ian said.

"Yes, many wild animals now. Look for dogs when we get out. They have gone wild," Vanko said. "Sometimes I bring scientists here. They study the plants and animals."

The horses wheeled away from the path parallel to the road and disappeared back into the forest like ghosts. The landscape looked totally different than the green forests I would sometimes find among my father's things; postcards and pictures scribbled with unknown letters, buried at the bottom of a drawer or imprisoned in the pages of a book.

We stopped just beyond the V.I. Lenin Nuclear Power Plant, where reactor number four slept uneasily under crumbling concrete and steel. Vanko got out of the car and tossed his cigarette down on the asphalt. He crushed it with his boot. We were in the ghost town, finally.

The last of the snow was melting away, leaving gray muddy puddles in the pitted streets. We walked into the town square. I turned and tried to see the power plant behind us. It was lost in the hazy air. Weeds slowly ate away at the roads, trees punched through the sidewalks, heaving slabs of pavement off. The buildings loomed in blind decrepitude; windows broken, paint peeling off, little more than shells now.

Other than our feet crunching across the concrete, it was quiet.

I visualized standing atop one of the crumbling tenement buildings and looking down upon the rusting, empty little corpse of a city; silent and alone, not even animals to break the apocalyptic scene.

"When first they brought people in to the area, they told them it was a fire," Vanko said. "They had no protection. They all died soon. This area is still poison. Dangerous to stay for long."

"Does anyone still live around here?" Ian asked. I stood next to him, the stiff leather sleeve of his jacket brushing my arm. I pulled my scarf up around my mouth and nose, breathing in the smell of fabric softener.

"Oh yes. Some would not leave. This is their home."

We walked across the square. I turned at each rustle, expecting dogs to set upon us, but I didn't see anything. It was just a wind stirring the grass. Vanko pointed out the Party Headquarters, its windows smashed out, jagged black holes in the icy surface of the glass. Ian took out a small notepad and scribbled down a few things.

"What do you think?" I asked.

"I think it looks like the end of the world. Wish I had brought my camera," he said.

"Do not go into the buildings," Vanko cautioned. "Very

contaminated there."

"But that's where I have to go," I said, pulling my scarf away from my mouth.

"Fine, go. I will not."

"Let me come with you," Ian said.

"You are both crazy. Not even thieves go in there anymore."

"Well, I'm going," I said, digging in my pocket for the paper where I'd written down which apartment I was looking for.

"I will wait by car. You hurry. I will not wait for long." Vanko threw up his hands and walked away.

"You don't have to come," I said, taking hold of Ian's arm.

"I want to," he said. He looked down at my hand. I pried my fingers off, wrapped my scarf around my mouth again and consulted my note. The buildings were in such disarray that it was difficult to find the numbers. We circled twice before we found the right one.

Inside, the floors were littered with broken glass, discarded objects, dust and paint chips. The walls were darkened to a sooty charcoal color. We pushed past a sapling growing out of the floor and continued toward the staircase. Third floor, second door on the right. The staircase creaked in protest.

"Look, here," Ian said, pointing out a collection of paper, faded photographs and broken glass that piled up against the walls of the hallway like a snowdrift. The building smelled of the damp and decaying plants. We found the door open and went in.

The room was tiny, smaller even than the room I was renting in town. On one wall, a calendar still dangled, the paper curled with moisture and the ink running into a blue blur.

"This is where your family used to live?" Ian asked, peering out the dirty window.

"It must be." I put on my leather gloves. "It's so small," I said. "It's hard to believe."

"What is?"

"That people once lived here. That they slept and cooked and felt safe in this room. Did they? Feel safe, I mean?" I turned and looked at him. His skin was white as a cave-dwelling creature against the darkness of the room. The grey cooling tower of the power plant was visible from here, just over Ian's shoulder. I tried to imagine having been here as a baby. My father, a younger version of the serious man I'd thought I knew. Of my mother, I could recover almost nothing. Saint Catherine in a radiation suit.

"I don't know," he said.

"Neither do I," I said and went to the closet, brushing dust and mushrooms out of the way. The acrid wet dirt smell made me cough. Ian knelt next to me and helped my brush away the debris. I felt for a loose board and found it, prying it up as best I could with my gloved fingers. A small piece of rotting wood studded with fungus came up in my hands. I threw it to the side.

Ian pulled a small flashlight out of his jacket and shined it down into the hole. There was a small rectangular shape there. I reached in and grabbed it. A box, probably cardboard, its print long obscured by the mildew that covered it. I tore off the lid and lifted a package from inside, a heavy little object wrapped in layers of cotton tied with string. I unwrapped it. It was the icon, a tiny golden painting, the square of wood that had expressed the faith of those who guarded it. It was something that had been believed. The light from Ian's flashlight illuminated the gold rays emanating from the portrait. The saint's huge eyes expressed an understanding that I envied. This square of wood, heavier than it seemed, was a small piece of a larger puzzle, an answer to a question I wasn't sure how to ask anymore. The saint's tiny painted mouth had no wisdom for me, but it was someplace to start.

"Is this it?" he asked.

"Yes. It's been with Zerovs for generations."

"It's beautiful," he said. I covered it with the wrappings and tucked it into my jacket.

"Let's get the fuck out of here," I said.

We made our way back down the stairs, breaking into a run at the entrance to the building. Ian stopped suddenly, grabbing me and holding me back. There was a soldier leisurely pissing against a tree just around the corner. He must have heard our feet scuffle to a top because he looked over his shoulder and shouted something. Another soldier emerged from the trees with his rifle aimed at both of us, barking commands. We froze.

They were different soldiers than the ones we had bribed to get into the zone. The pissing one was fat and red-faced, probably drunk, while the other was meaty like a bull with almost no discernable neck. I'd stupidly left behind my dictionary. With these two men now pointing guns in our faces, I wished I'd had that dictionary so I could have at least attempted some excuse.

"Fuck," Ian said as they turned us to the left and jabbed us in the back with their guns, forcing us to walk away from the square and into the trees. Brambles of dormant berry branches snagged my clothes. They pushed me up against a tree, the cracks in the bark black and scented with wet decay. They laughed and I smelled harsh cigarette smoke. In my peripheral vision I could see the other soldier searching Ian. My face was forced down as the soldier's gloved hands went into my pockets, unzipped my jacket and then dipped to the icon. He stepped back and examined the package, tossing off the wrappings.

"No." I turned and reached for it. The soldier sneered and moved with practiced cruelty and I felt a stinging heat rising to my face. My legs gave out and I was on the ground and I didn't know why until the heat spread down my neck and I touched the spot and my hand came away with slick redness and I puked into the leaf mold.

"Leave her alone," I could hear Ian shout, but it was dim, as from a long distance away. The soldiers laughed. I looked up. The one who'd struck me pulled off my scarf and wiped the butt of his rifle with it, tossing the bloodied strip away like a used bandage. He smiled at me and slid the icon into his overcoat. They shoved Ian toward me and walked away into the forest. Ian helped me to my feet.

"You can't take that," I said, as if that would make it true.

"I can pay you. Fucking assholes. I have money." They seemed to understand enough of Ian's shouting to take offense. The red-faced one blew a plume of vodka-scented breath in my face as he struck me again with his gloved fist. My hand tightened around Ian's arm, but I felt him being pulled away and was left on my own failing legs. A huge hand on my shoulder and I was down on my knees in the remnants of my breakfast.

Everything tilted away. A bright pain flared in my head, suffusing the forest with harsh light. I was vaguely aware of being on the ground. In the center of my vision, I saw a shape coming toward me—a dark figure sucking in all the light. Not either of the soldiers, I realized as the shape filled out, stretched to take up every inch of space. More like a huge absence shaped like a figure. An inverted St. Catherine, a messenger bearing a void instead of the light. Voices dripped into this airless space from a vast distance as I felt myself falling toward a darkness that was more complete, more final than any night. Cries that seemed uncannily familiar, though distant now, left me vaguely aware that the soldiers were still there, hurting someone. I had no awareness at that time that the cries I was hearing were my own. The darkness was fascinating, impossible to turn away from. It was a rift that reached into the forest, malevolently drawing everything down into itself. The darkness contracted into a figure again, appeared to move to my side. It reached out to me, black finger-shapes extending like wisps of smoke drawn out a window.

Pain wound itself tightly around my ribs as the soldier kicked me. I fought closing my eyes, afraid of what other things awaited in that space. The darkness was close. I couldn't see it but I could feel it—a heavy presence that settled over me. My lungs emptied. My arms and legs refused to move, no matter how I commanded myself to fight back. It must have happened then. I felt something like taking a deep inhalation of ice water—a long cold penetration.

Ian's voice snapped into focus. Coughing. They'd subdued him, but saved the best of their efforts for me.

"Jesus Christ," Ian said, and helped me up. I vomited again, thin streaks of blood coloring the forest floor. "Come on, Maryska, we have to," he said, putting his arm around my waist. I tried to talk, but only a sputtering sound came out. Pain knifed down my neck, sending a wave of unconsciousness up to meet me.

I recall driving off at such a speed I thought the car would shake itself to rust flakes before we got back to town. I could open my eyes a little by then. Ian peeled off his gloves, tossed them out the window, tore off a piece of the white t-shirt he'd worn under his sweater and pressed it to my face. With every breath I felt something shifting inside me, something that seemed to grow heavier with every heartbeat.

"You both need decontamination shower," Vanko shouted over the laboring of the engine.

"Fuck you," Ian said. Vanko cursed vehemently in Russian. "You're going to be fine."

I could feel blood soaking through the cloth. Pain was spreading through my skull. By the time we got to a doctor, the cloth was stiffening with dried blood.

"I'm sorry," I remember Ian whispering before the weight inside me dragged me back into unconsciousness.

The scar left on my face felt puckered and snaked from the corner of my lip like a permanent snarl. My jaw had to be wired shut. I had broken ribs, a broken ankle and a patchwork of bruises. They wouldn't let me leave the hospital because of the radiation I'd gotten from touching things in the ghost town. At least, that's what they told me. No one asked where I'd gotten the wounds. No one cared.

It wasn't until I was able to find a mirror that I saw the darkness again. At first I avoided thinking about my face, but I finally decided I had to know how bad it was. One of the nurses brought me a mirror, but didn't stay around after handing it off to me. I assumed this meant the damage to my face was bad enough that she wouldn't be able to fake any reassurance.

At first I thought it was a problem with my eyes, or perhaps damage to my brain that caused me to see a vague black shape where my reflection should be. But the mirror clearly showed me the rest of the room, even the blanket I pulled up to my nose. It was only my hands, my face that were erased, completely blacked-out in the mirror-image. I remember how my hands shook as I placed the mirror carefully down. A thrum like the vibration of hundreds of bee's wings went through me and I could feel the heaviness in my chest flex and relax like a satisfied cat.

Ian stayed with me, visiting me when he could and contacting the American Embassy to help me get home as soon as possible. Ian made appropriate bribes for me. He blamed himself, and he pitied me, that much was clear even if he couldn't bring himself to say so. The soldiers had made him watch while they'd taken turns kicking me. Perhaps they hadn't thought he was a threat. Or maybe there was just something about me that made them choose me instead of him. In the end, I had to convince him it didn't matter. That trying to find reasons for what happened was pointless.

I wanted to tell him about the mirror and the darkness then, but I had no words for it. I thought it would go away. That like my imaginings of Saint Catherine and my father's life, this would fade, a misconception that time could wipe clean.

But the darkness remained to blot out my image, no matter how much time passed.

On the day they released me I traveled with Ian to the airport in Kiev. It still hurt some to talk. I sat close to him on the bus and wrote on a notepad with a pencil.

Something about the day we went to the ghost town, I wrote.
"Yes?"

I saw something then. I shifted so that I was angled away from the black reflection of myself in the window. Since I'd discovered the change in me, I kept my back to reflective surfaces. The void shape in the reflection terrified me. I feared that if I looked at it too long, it would start to move of its own volition.

"What was it?" He held my hand. Behind us, a pair of teenagers giggled.

I moved the pencil over the paper. He read it. "Are you serious?" His hand squeezed mine tighter.

Out the window, the cold roadside ditches snaked past. And as I began to pull the sheet off the notepad, I knew the words on the page were wrong, but as close as I might ever get to the truth.

A black hole, in the shape of a man, they said.

When She Wakes Up

Angela finishes lacing her boots, adds another handful of mousse to her pink hair and goes out into the hallway. Outside her sister's door, she stops. There is a little light coming through the cracks, sentimentally golden. Without looking in, Angela knows the glow will be coming from a hundred white candles, stiflingly perfumed and somber in their little dresses of light. And encircled in candlelight will be Rosalyn, her sister, still on her bed of rosy flowered sheets with an army of wet-eyed saints looking over her. Angela's hand pauses before turning the knob. Today she'd heard her mother saying the word *Beatified* on the phone and she could not believe it was her sister that was being spoken of.

"Angie."

"I was just," she begins to protest.

"Shhh, don't bother Rosie."

Angela turns to the shadow of her mother at the bottom of the stairs. She feels the hot and holy breath of her sister's room and imagines the damp relief of the air outside. The plush carpet beneath her rubber soles traps the heavy perfumes of the house: urine, wax, and roses. Her mother ascends the stairs and opens the door.

"It"s late. What are you doing?" Angela's mother busies herself at Rosalyn's bedside. Her sister's long blonde hair lies across the pillow. Her eyes are open to a crescent of senseless white and a drop of drool caresses the corner of her slack mouth. Arrayed throughout the room are statuettes and paintings; Christ with his raw heart exposed like some lecher opening his coat and the Virgin Mary's dispassionate mouth. The statues have little white dishes underneath them to catch the tears and holy oil that they issue from their plaster eyes. And in the center of this galaxy of mercy, her sister, inert as the plaster statues should be. The machine that breathes for Rosalyn snores mechanically. *The Slumbering Saint*, the devout call her, though she isn't technically asleep.

"Whatever you're up to I expect proper behavior from you tomorrow while Father Conti is here." Angela's mother checks the tube that drains the urine from Rosalyn's body.

"I'm going out." Every inch of the dresser along the wall is covered with weeping statues and prayer cards sent from all over the world. All the hearts and blood and martyrdom make it look more like a shrine to horror films.

"Not tonight. We're going to follow the Stations of the Cross on TV."

Angela sighs loudly. Holy oil and disinfectant heated in the intolerable closeness of the room assault her nose. She is tired of the strangers praying on the front lawn and the Catholic freak show. Her mother drowns herself in piety to cope with Roslyn's condition since her father left four years ago; off to make a new family since this one turned out so fucked up.

"I need to go," Angela says.

Her mother puts on a mask of exhaustion. "Angie."

"No. I have to get away from this."

Angela slams the door of her sister's room behind her and stomps down the stairs. She pushes past another candlelit vigil to her friend's waiting car.

The worn plush of the Lincoln's back seat presses comfortingly against Angela's back. The windows are down and the bad stereo plays music of careless darkness. Cigarette smoke fills her mouth and lungs as Leah searches in her coat for the acid she's brought. Angela watches the warped night-reflection of her face in the window. Her face disappears when they pass a streetlight, only to resurface like a fish coming up to feed as the car rolls through the darkness. Bramble curses someone from behind the driver's wheel.

"Calm down, sweetness, we'll get there before the booze runs out," Gareth purrs. Bramble smacks him and he takes her hand and kisses it.

"Ah, here it is, finally," Leah says once the hidden

hallucinogenic treasure has been found. "Want half?" she asks Angela.

"No thanks, I'll see what they've got at the party."

"Your mom was okay with you coming out?" Gareth asks.

"No. But she can't stop me anyway."

"My mom was all blah blah today about how I shouldn't be drinking or whatever. I told her we were all just going to play board games tonight..." Leah's voice continues on but Angela is watching her face float in the window like the magic mirror in *Snow White*.

To the lullaby of engine and wheels and the warmth of Leah's arm in its warm leather jacket pressing against her, Angela tells herself this story:

Once upon a time there was a princess, blonde and pretty of course, since princess genes are just like that. They make the kind of girls who are called *delicate*. Anyway, the princess gets herself cursed, and time and the world stop for her. She gets an extended nap, and everyone waits for her slumber to end, so they can serve her once again. The king and queen freeze in their souls, and the princess' sister is trapped in this timelessness, and only she continues to live while everyone around her stops. But what if the prince never shows up to give the reanimating kiss? Then, when does the world start again? *But there's a big difference*, a voice that sounds a lot like her sister's used to cuts in. *You can still walk away, can't you?*

They arrive at the party, a small crowded house with more cars than lawn.

"Gareth, get me a drink," Bramble says, pointing an imperious finger into the kitchen.

There are few faces Angela recognizes. A crowd has congregated around the television, watching a muted Kung-Fu film. On the screen, a luminescent rain of green leaves falls on a woman in a white kimono. She holds her sword at the throat of a man in black and red. Their long, dark hair commingles, the wind braiding it together.

"Bramble, Angela, I'm glad you could make it." The hostess emerges from the kitchen. "There's tons of liquor in the kitchen, and plastic cups, and ice, and some food. Oh, Larry's monopolizing the stereo right now, but we can change the music if you brought any CDs."

"We'll save the Smiths until Bram is nicely weepy drunk," Gareth says, reappearing between them.

"Shut up, bitch." She grabs her drink from him and goes down the hall.

Gareth shrugs and hands Angela a red plastic cup.

"What's in it?"

"Good stuff," he says.

Angela sniffs the liquid. It smells like peaches, cherry candy and alcohol.

"Aren't we just lubricant in the machine of juvenile delinquency?" Sara pokes Gareth in the ribs. He smiles his carnivorous smile; the smooth gesture oiled with lust that Angela privately calls his Please-Fuck-Me-Smile. *He probably thinks he can get me drunk enough to get lucky again. Not tonight.* She escapes to the porch and lights another cigarette.

The night air is warm and scented with orange blossom and chlorinated water from the neighbor's pool. She sits in one of the flimsy plastic chairs. Three people she's never met before are talking and she gathers it has something to do with a concert they went to last night. Angela turns herself slightly away from them in her chair. She doesn't want to seem like she's trying to intrude on the conversation. From where she sits, she can see the white kimono woman on the TV flying up through the branches of a huge tree, her black hair whipping around like a raven banner. Her sister used to make her play Rapunzel with her. Rosalyn spent twenty minutes tying long strands of yarn around her ponytail. Then, once she had a long rope of yellow acrylic hair, she'd climb up on top of the tall dresser they had to share with the hair draped over her arm like a lasso. Angela's job was then to be the prince and beg Rosalyn to let her hair down. While Angela called out her request, Rosalyn pretended to comb the hair. Rosalyn rarely let the hair down on the first request. Angela was supposed to beg louder and louder for the beautiful princess to let her hair down. Once Rosalyn tossed down the yarn hair, Angela was supposed to climb up but not pull the hair hard enough for it to fall out. She often got this part wrong. Either she pulled too hard and the hair came tumbling down onto her or she couldn't keep hold of the hair while she pulled herself up on the dresser. Angela never got to be Rapunzel. Whenever she asked why, Rosalyn explained that she was the older sister so she got to pick who was Rapunzel. End of story.

The white kimono woman makes a slashing motion with her arm and from somewhere off the screen a spray of blood arcs onto the silk like cherries on a bough, red on white. Angela tastes the drink. It is syrupy sharp like the kiss of an enemy. In Rosalyn's room there is red and white. Saint Sebastian's pale face and chest, with the ribbons of blood pinned to his flesh like military medals. The eyes of Saint Bernadette upturned so white in their ecstasy.

One of the three people, a guy with a ratty ponytail of faded blue hair turning to green at the tips, turns to Angela and extends his hand. She doesn't want to seem rude, so she shakes his hand. The other two burst out laughing.

"Nice to meet you too, pinky, but I wanted you to hand me that ashtray over there."

Angela hands him the heavy glass ashtray. He seems older than her, but she can't tell by how much. One of his legs is crossed over the other and in the gap between his cut off army shorts and his combat boots, a slice of pale, hairy leg is visible. The leg seems far too thin and reminds Angela of her sister's limbs as they are manipulated by the physical therapist that comes to combat Rosalyn's muscle atrophy.

"Oh, don't be like that. I was just joshing." He says *joshing* as though it's the punch line to a joke. "I'm Finn. It's okay, I won't bite. Unless you ask very nicely."

"Angela," she says.

"What are you drinking?" He takes the cup out of her hand and sniffs it. The chains pinned all over his leather jacket jingle as he moves. "Smells like a Scarlet O'Hara. You like this stuff?"

"It's all right." Angela takes the cup back.

"Kids," he says to the other two. "Come on, you can sit closer."

Angela moves her chair a few inches closer. He smells like leather, clove cigarettes and patchouli. A scent she knows well; most of her black-eyeliner crowd wears it. She takes a sip of the drink and though the sugary liquid makes her teeth hurt, she smiles to deflect further mockery.

"Who are you here with?"

"Bramble, Gareth. They're in there." She points into the house.

"Oh yeah. How come I haven't seen you before?"

"Because." She shrugs. She imagines she could sound mysterious. "I just popped into existence tonight. Before that, I was living in a very tall tower."

"What?" He seems confused.

"Forget it. A joke."

"You two look nice together," one of the others says, lighting a candle in a blue hurricane glass. "Blue and pink. You'll have purple-haired little kids."

Finn leans back and looks at Angela in mock-seriousness.

"Do you enjoy long walks along a moonlit post-nuclear beach? The fallout is such a lovely color when the moon is full."

"Yeah, I'm out of here," the candle-lighter announces. "You're getting all weird again."

"What? What did I say?" Finn asks.

"Come on Craig, let's go get more beer."

With a slide of the glass door Angela is alone with Finn. She drinks three big gulps so she'll have something to do other than talk.

"Don't mind them. Inside joke."

"There seem to be a lot of jokes in the air tonight, but no laughs." Angela stands.

84

"Where are you going? Am I not charming enough for you?"

"I should find my friends."

"Sit down. I know your friends. They're boring and self-absorbed. Has anyone ever read your palm?"

"My what?"

"Your palm." He reaches for her hand and clasps it, turning the palm up. "Trust me. I'm a shaman."

Angela sits, resigning herself to at least two minutes of nonsense before she can use needing the bathroom as an excuse to break away. She finishes her drink and sets the hollow plastic cup down.

"Okay."

Finn scoots to the edge of his seat, intent on her hand. His hand is warm on hers. A vapor of whiskey drifts on his breath as he exhales. Their heads are bent close together as they look down onto the lines of her hand in the candlelight.

"Kind of hard to see," he mutters. Her hand looks like the ocean floor with the blue light cast by the candle washing over it. "Soft hands. Well, your lifeline is well formed. That's good. Means you won't have a long illness in your life."

No, not mine, she thinks. No one could have foreseen the pool accident that took Rosalyn from them. They'd both had swimming lessons. It seems like it only took a fraction of a moment. Angela had gone inside for a popsicle. The only one left was lime. Rosalyn loved the cherry ones as much as Angela did and often got the last one. The taste of that vitriolic lime ice melting in her mouth as she returned to the pool puckered her cheeks. Angela cursing her sister for taking the last cherry one. Rosalyn's blonde hair floating like seaweed. Angela stood at the edge of the pool, her teeth digging into the nasty lime popsicle for ten, twenty seconds before she realized something was wrong.

"Nice Mount of Venus," he says, pressing the fleshy pad just under her thumb. He leaned forward as if in anticipation.

"What?"

"Sorry. Bad joke. Anyway, your heart line and your head

line sharply diverge, here. That means you could have some trouble later with your feelings pulling you in the opposite direction from what your head wants."

"Okay." Angela wanted to tell him that he could be describing anyone, but she waited to see if he came up with anything more original.

"But this is totally weird. Your line of fate. It looks like it branches off." He leaned closer, the chains on his jacket chiming as he did.

"What does that mean?"

"Well, it's your life path. You have two. Freaky. Just here, see? The line splits off to form another line at an angle. A little tangent."

"So what?"

"I've never heard of that. It's like you're responsible for two fates."

A short bark of a laugh comes out her mouth then because she knows it's true. She has been responsible for two fates. She can still feel the cold, wet tiles at the pool's edge under her feet as her teeth dig into the frozen lime popsicle. She lets her sister float for—how long?—while imagining how good that cherry one would have tasted. And even worse, when she returns there now she imagines she could have sat down with her feet dangling into the pool and finished her lime popsicle before finding her mother and telling her Rosalyn wasn't moving. She could have stopped it all back then; unraveled the story before the princess could even fall into her accursed sleep.

"What if I am?" Her voice is barely audible over the laughter coming from inside the house. Her breaths come in sobs.

"You going to be okay?"

"No, I don't think so."

Angela pulls the glass door open and lurches into the house. A blast of recirculated air sets the hair on her arms on end.

"Had one too many?" someone asks.

Her stomach churns up the syrupy drink. She braces herself on the arm of the couch and stumbles away to the bathroom.

Angela vomits into the pale porcelain bowl. She leans against the coolness of the bathtub while she waits for the next wave of nausea to grip her. On the door, a full-length mirror reflects her, slumped on the floor, a mass of pink and black. Angela vomits again, grateful that she has no long hair to guard from the spewing bile. Her arms are too weak to even hold her up. She feels a warm, dry hand on the back of her neck. She turns, expecting Finn, but in the mirror, a tall, blonde girl is standing over her, caressing her with holy mercy.

"Angela," she says.

The girl in the mirror, the girl Angela knows will be gone if she turns around is radiantly white and gold. Her hair rains down in scintillating Pre-Raphaelite profusion. Rapunzel's hair, real now.

"I'm here," she says.

"I'm hallucinating," Angela tells the mirror. She looks exactly like Angela has always imagined Rosalyn would look.

"If only. You know me, don't try to rationalize now. How many conversations have we had before now?"

"I can't deal right now."

"I appreciate your distress, but it's a little unnecessary. I'll live."

Angela laughs bitterly, choking on the taste of acid.

"I never was able to rescue you from the tower. Why did you keep making me be the prince?"

"Maybe I knew you'd find another way."

"Another way for what?"

"Break the spell." The girl sweeps her platinum hair over her shoulder. She's so white it hurts to look at her, even in the mirror.

"How the hell can I do that? I can't change what happened." Angela tries to wipe away the black smudges around her eyes.

"You think you're the only one who wishes you hadn't found me when you did?"

"I don't know."

"If I had a voice, it wouldn't sound like a respirator pump. I need you to find the answer, Angela. After all," the girl replies,

"I'm only the Rosalyn that would have been, *your* Rosalyn, free of that corpse. I'm only a maybe that never happened."

"I can't take it anymore. They're going to bring in a priest, to validate your miracles. Do you have any idea how much that sucks? My own sister continues to upstage me, even comatose."

The girl stands, stretches and turns. "Think of everything you have, Angela. To even be able to walk, or move, or to listen, I don't have that. Remember that first cigarette, the first one you *really* wanted, or that night with Gareth. The red candles, remember? I'll never have that."

"Rosie, please, just tell me. The oils, the crying Jesus' and shit, that's really just you, isn't it? It's not God, it's you trying to scream from in there."

"It's hard to say. My mind is lost in so much water these days."

"Damn it, please."

"You can still walk away, can't you?"

Angela turns and she is gone. The light is going out in the small bathroom. An electrical pop and the lightbulb dies, dropping the room into black. Someone pounds on the door. It is Bramble.

"Come out, it's okay."

Not really, she thinks and rinses her mouth out with water.

On the way home, with Leah driving because she's the only one who didn't drink, and she can drive while tripping—as she constantly reminds them—Angela tells herself this story:

Once upon a time there was a princess who was cursed, and so she fell asleep, and was taken prisoner in her own body. And the saints in her room wept endless ephemeral tears. The king and queen, who had frozen in their souls, called these tears miracles. But only the sister of the princess knew her secret. Those tears were hers, because though so much of her was dead, her spirit lived, and tried to call out to her sister. And all the stopped people sang the song of the princess' glory, sure to return when she woke up. They waited, statues of their former selves, for the one who would come to break the spell. But the princess' sister knew that would never happen. It would never, ever happen.

Angela sneaks up the stairs. The house is silent. Darkness issues from the doorway of Rosalyn's room. Angela goes to her room and dumps the books out of her backpack. She refills it with clothes and the money she has been stashing for a car. In Rosalyn's room, Angela lights one votive to see by. Her sister is waxen in its light, an effigy.

Angela kneels at the closet and pushes the door open. She finds a shoebox and brings it out. Inside lays a ragged doll, one of the last artifacts from Rosalyn's waking days. The doll is soaked through with a slick, light fluid. Her hands shake. This thing has cried Rosalyn's tears too.

The machines hum an endless lullaby. Angela touches the pearl rosary around her sister's neck. It has been warmed by her body. Rosalyn's eyelids flicker: a random muscle movement, a doctor once explained when Angela asked if Rosalyn was dreaming. Angela closes her eyes, trying to imagine a downy blackness surrounding her, dreamless and binding and timeless. Suspended like a fly in a spider's web. In church they told her purgatory was like that. A big nothingness in which you floated, waiting for the day when you could arise to heaven. It sounded like hell to her.

Angela puts the doll in Rosalyn's bed and kisses her sister on the forehead. Rosalyn twitches slightly, reacting perhaps to an involuntary spasm. Angela has seen her live in the confines of this bed for eleven years. She closes the door and locks it. Her hand seeks out the plug that keeps the respirator running. The cord is smooth and innocuous beneath her fingers. One would hardly believe that this little bit of plastic fed life into another human being. Angela knows there can be no staying in this house once she does this. She will return to the party, maybe try to find Finn. The machine sucks in air as though holding its own breath. A sharp tug and the machine goes silent.

When she opens the window a rush of air scented with orange blossoms blows out the candle.

Beauty Asleep

Elise was asleep. From where he sat at the edge of the bed, Morris felt the heat radiating from her unconscious body, even through the sheets. There had been another argument that morning. He had committed the unspeakable crime of forgetting to empty the dishwasher. The rage that dripped form her mouth hit him like hailstones.

But in their bedroom, all was silent and still. Her face pressed into the blue pillowcase; luminous against the dark cloth like a cloud pinned to the twilight. Morris reached out to tuck a strand of her hair behind her ear. The touch sent a ripple of partial-awareness through her. She turned slightly away and groaned. Even in her sleep, she seemed to be angry with him.

That day Morris had been working on the new Lunairen campaign. The others at the agency had been brainstorming sleep, dreams, what kept people up at night. Morris tapped his pencil on the table and thought about the way Elise slept—with her mouth open just a bit so that her teeth glinted out from between her lips when the light from the bathroom was on. Next to him, Katie filled her notepad with words contained in bubbles. *Lullaby. Sleep. River. Pillow. Feather. Moth.* Tyson suggested a Sleeping Beauty type of story.

"But instead of waking her up, maybe the prince brings Beauty some Lunairen," Tyson said, carefully holding his pen at either end and turning it slowly.

"Because she's an insomniac?" Katie suggested.

"And then she can sleep happily ever after." Tyson turned toward Morris. "What do you think?"

He envisioned the prince mounting the stone stairs–because that's what a prince does, he can't just step as purposelessly as the rest of them–his armor shining silver and clean in a dreamy violet half-light. The princess in her bed. Her hair tangled with tossing, her eyes red at the edges. A petulant sigh that betrays her exhaustion.

"I can do some concept sketches today," Morris said.

He'd been awakened early that morning by the sound of dishes clattering into the cabinets. Elise cursed and slammed the dishwasher shut. The bedroom door flung open and she stood in the doorway in nothing but a pair of pink leopard-print panties with a small hole just over the left side of her hip. A mug with its handle broken off was in her hand. She started yelling about her favorite mug and how this wouldn't happen if he could remember to put the dishes away and not make her do everything, but all he could focus on were the orange numbers on the alarm clock and how they were two hours behind what they should be for him to be awake. Elise started crying, slammed the door behind her. Morris knew this was his cue to chase her until she turned a firehose of verbal abuse on him. Incompetent lazy shit that he was, he peeled the covers off and went after her.

Back at his desk he made several versions of the sleepless princess. Blonde, innocent, waifish. One a Pre-Raphaelite brunette. A nervous-looking redhead. But the prince was still a blank in his mind. Just a pair of riding boots and chiming silver armor rising step by step toward the princess' chamber.

At home, Morris made sure to put his socks in the dirty clothes hamper. Elise always hated it when he left them on the floor. Especially when the goddamn hamper was two fucking feet away for fuck's sake. He pulled back the sheets and slid into bed next to her. The streetlight leaked in at the edges of the blinds, casting a chemical yellow glow over his wallet and keys on the dresser. Elise turned away from him, and he moved closer to her, slipping his hand over her waist. Her hair was in his face, almost chokingly up his nose and covering his mouth with its hairsprayed stiffness and afterscent of peroxide. Morris watched the sticky strands of her hair made luminous by the errant streetlight rise and fall slightly with her breath. He closed his eyes and imagined that their room was the sleeping princess' chamber, magically lush with the invading tendrils of vines. They would be visited at night by glowing clouds of white moths, their fluttering wings stirring a breeze that smoothed Elise's hair against the pillow. And while she slept, her face would be as calm and lovely as—not the moon. That was too expected. What else, he wondered. A stone. River. Feather. Moth.

Elise was already at work by the time Morris woke up the next day. He'd slept through the alarm again. Usually, Elise elbowed him until he realized that the alarm was going off. But she'd started a new shift at the flower shop and had to be there early enough to get the deliveries. Morris shut off the robotic beep of the alarm and hauled himself to the shower. He made it to the office thirty minutes late, which really didn't seem to phase Tyson, since he was the sort of manager who thought creative people could be forgiven a number of quirks as long as they were good at what he paid them to do. Morris was about to start a new sketch of the princess for the Lunairen campaign when Katie leaned over his desk.

"So, have you ever read any of this?" She held up a book by the Brothers Grimm, keeping her place with one finger.

"Maybe. Like, when I was a kid or something."

"Yeah, well, this is some twisted shit," she sat down on Morris' desk, crumpling one of his previous sketches with her ass as she wiggled herself back. Morris wanted to reach for the page, but didn't want Katie to think he was trying to touch her ass. He picked up a koosh ball and played with that instead. Above her head, a tiny white blur dashed itself repeatedly against the fluorescent light.

"In the original Sleeping Beauty story, the prince is kind of a date-rapist."

"What do you mean?" Morris dug his fingers into the rubbery strands of the toy, which were the same shade of blue as Katie's toenails; not more than a few feet from his face as she unselfconsciously bounced her leg while she spoke.

"Well, he makes his way into the tower and all that, only he does a lot more to the princess than just kiss her. He fucks her and prances off on his merry way. Only later after she has a pair of baby Prince Juniors one of them sucks the magical splinter out of her finger and that's what wakes her up."

Katie closed the book and gave Morris a look as though waiting for a reaction to a joke. But all he could think of was the armor and the fabric of the princess's dress; the metal tearing through with ease. Then, of what was underneath. Skin on steel. Bruises. Rips. The cloudy bed in tatters.

"We can't use any of that," he said, tossing the ball back onto the desk.

"It's kind of sexy in a gross Freudian way," she said. Above her head the insect circled and crashed again into the light.

"I'm not drawing that." Gray steel, pink satin. Pink and soft and silken. Morris imagined the prince's spurs tearing into the mattress. White feathers drifting down to the floor like snowflakes.

Katie shrugged and slid off the desk. The paper she'd been sitting on fell to the floor, slightly crumpled and still warm from having been underneath her. Morris straightened the page against his desk. He studied the princess' face—little more than a few lines, really—for any hint that betrayed her knowledge of what was to come. Would she know what that inexorable beat of riding boots on the steps was bringing her?

The insect fell to the page, its filmy white wings almost translucent against the paper. Tiny holes dotted the wings, which flexed convulsively as if to say *Not yet, there's a bit of pain left in me still*. Morris gently brushed the moth off the page, then crushed it with his thumb.

Morris dropped his keys into the bowl Elise had designated for that purpose. The gunfire tattoo of Elise's sewing machine beat under the hum of the air conditioner. He followed the sound of the machine to their spare room, which held both Elise's sewing supplies and his canvases. She leaned close to the machine, the tiny light over the needle illuminating a strand of red thread clinging to her bleached-blonde bangs. Shreds of pale fabric cut from thrift-store t-shirts sat next to the machine. Elise's huge steel scissors lay on the floor next to her bare foot.

"I want to make out with you," he said.

The staccato noise of the machine stopped.

"Are you fucking sixteen or something?"

"You used to say I was a good kisser."

"Morris." She bent to the machine and the needle punched through the strips of fabric, leaving a scar of red thread. A circle of light illuminated the lotus tattooed on her wrist. Morris wanted to take her hair out of its ponytail and run his hands through it while pressing his semi-erection into her back.

Elise turned away from the machine and took up the scissors. She began to cut more shirts into the strips. The scissors' steel jaws pivoted silently as the shirts came undone.

"You're hovering," she said without looking up.

Morris leaned his hip against the doorway. He had always admired how Elise took these shreds of someone else's discarded nostalgia—shirts with trucking company logos, bands that had once mattered, defunct little leagues—and remade them. As she worked, the strips fell to the floor, curling at the cut edges.

"Listen, I have a ton of work to do and I'm already so far behind. We had a big funeral thing today for some politician's son who strangled himself while jacking off. Plus, this chick has already paid me for this dress and as you can plainly see," she gestured around her to the piles of fabric, "it's not done."

A strip of fabric fell away from the shirt in Elise's hand and fell limp to the floor. The material was worn almost sheer and Morris thought of the moth; the strips of fabric like its shredded wings. He wondered if Elise could remake that too; take the thin material and stretch it over some gossamer frame that would have allowed the moth an escape.

"Didn't you miss me today?"

"If I don't have this ready tomorrow morning, I'm done. Plus I'm probably only getting three hours of sleep tonight. And you forgot to load the dishwasher again. I can't do everything around here."

She gathered up the shreds of fabric and dropped them next to her machine. Morris hesitated at the threshold of the room. He wanted to come in, hold her, inhale her scent of peroxide, hairspray and pollen; take her hand and push it down the front of his pants. Elise shook her head as she piled the new strips on the old ones. She gave a sharp cry and pulled her hand away.

At first, Morris thought the needle had gone all the way through the nail on the other side. Elise's face went waxen and ugly. The needle stuck out of the finger like and arrow quivering in a tree trunk. There was an awful tension in the angle of the needle and Morris thought it must surely be embedded straight into the bone. There was an instant sympathetic pain in his own hand as he watched Elise squeeze her wrist.

"Pull. It. Out," she gasped. Her eyes had gone red and her lips curled back from her teeth.

The idea of touching the needle—feeling it stuck fast in the bone—made Morris sick in his stomach. Elise's mouth gaped, the lips bloodless and quivering as she held her wrist with her other hand. He tried to remember if it had been a needle that had done in Sleeping Beauty too, but Elise was wailing and sobbing and overreacting as she did anytime she was injured.

"What the fuck are you waiting for," she cried.

Morris grasped the needle and tugged. He swallowed down a twinge of pain as the needle slipped free, drawing a bead of ruby blood with it. Elise stuck the injured finger into her mouth.

"I . . ."

"Get out." Elise said, the finger now sucked clean of blood.

He wanted to tell her about the pain; how he'd felt it too

and that was why he couldn't pull out the needle right away. But Elise had already turned away from him and was kicking stray bits of fabric out of her way. Morris watched the birds tattooed on her shoulders flutter as she shook her hand for a moment longer, then he retreated back to the kitchen.

The bloody needle burned like ice between his fingers. He dropped it into the trash. By the keys in the bowl lay his portfolio of sketches for Lunairen. Morris pulled out the pages of sleeping princesses. Their mouths in closed repose, their hair spread in smooth waves over the pillows. He sketched in a few tiny details even though he knew they would never make it into the final ad. By the princess' bed he added a pincushion porcupined with needles. On another princess he added the suggestion of a tattoo on her wrist.

The sewing machine resumed its beat. Morris slid the sketches back into the folder and started making dinner. As he reached for the basil, he brushed aside a packet of allergy pills and paused. Elise sometimes took them during bouts of insomnia. She often lay in the bed next to him tense as a coil of wire, her feet touching his as she shifted in search of elusive comfort. The sewing machine let off another burst of fire. Morris knew that Elise would be up tending the machine all night. He slept poorly without her hair in his face and the pressure of her body on the mattress near him. Morris popped three pink pills out of the plastic blisters and crushed them into a fine powder with the back of a spoon. The powder went into a cup of tomato sauce that he would later pour over Elise's portion of ravioli. And when she said she wouldn't have time for dinner, Morris would bring her the bowl in the spare room and watch from the doorway until all the red tomato sauce disappeared past her pale lips.

When all the tensions of the day make sleep seem like a fairy-tale, there's Lunairen. Lunairen helps you fall asleep fast and wake refreshed and ready to face the world again. Lunairen has a special time-release formula that ensures a deep, restful sleep with no lingering morning grogginess. Not all patients react well to Lunairen. Side effects may include nausea, headache, night-time activities that one has no memory of, unexplained punctures on the hands, cessation of temporal movement, birth of twin aristocrats, and living unhappily ever after.

Ask your doctor about Lunairen. The beauty of sleep.™

Morris found her curled under the machine. The half-finished dress lay in her lap; a mass of off-white rags veined with red thread. Elise had been embroidering a panel in the center of the dress with snaking lines of red stitching and they reminded Morris of the veins you saw if you put your hand over a flashlight. He rested his hand on the warm plastic casing before switching the sewing machine off and heaving Elise up. They were about the same size, so it wasn't easy for him to carry her, but he managed to get her to the bed. Her breaths were deep and even, a steady rising and falling of her chest even as he stripped her. Her arms and legs were as limp as the strips of fabric she used in her dresses. He had some trouble getting everything off, but finally she lay naked and still. Morris combed some of the stiffness out of her hair and arranged it on the pillow before pulling the sheet over her. Her eyelashes formed a dark crescent under her eyes, like reverse moons reflecting the darkness of the night instead of the salvaged light of day. Morris took off his sneakers and got onto the bed next to her. He took her finger and inspected the site of the wound. There was little more than a tiny hole, already turning reddish violet at the edges. Morris held his own hand to hers for comparison, half-expecting to see a matching mark of his own. There was nothing there.

He put his hand over her throat and felt her pulse beating. Her face was slack and peaceful. As blank as the princesses he'd drawn. He would watch her sleep all night, Morris resolved. He would guard her in this vulnerability. Keep her at peace.

There were three of them at first. The blonde frosty and gorgeous but without the sharp edge of knowledge in her eyes. The brunette with the androgynous angle of her jaw and meltingly dark eyes. The redhead sprinkled with freckles that gave her a fawnish look. They emerged out of a fog. Morris realized that he can see no more than an arm's span in any direction. The three surrounded him and they were his whole world. There was no sound but the in and out of their breaths, their pleasant sighs, a sibilant rustle of their gowns which appear to be sewn out of fragile shreds of silk. They pressed against him, hands slipping his shirt off, hands touching his lips, insistently tugging down his pants. A feminine scent of flowers and hair and sugar invaded his lungs with each indrawn breath. Three smiles, six jewel-like eyes. Pairs of hands stroked his skin. Like falling into a warm bath, Morris surrendered to the women. He closed his eyes and realized that there were too many hands on him for three women and when he opened them again he saw endless replicas of his three princesses rising out of the mist. Morris, surrounded by a crush of princesses, looked more closely at the fog and became aware that it was not a mist but rather a cloud of the tiniest white moths he had ever seen. The women displayed flashing smiles as they touched him, their fingers digging more aggressively into his flesh. There were hands all over his body, tugging, gripping, making him wonder how long he could stand under this erotic onslaught. Their lips pressed to his neck, soft flesh holding him tight. Morris felt a tongue questing into his mouth. The princesses inhaled and exhaled as one, their breaths coming heavier as they pulled at him.

The sharpness of a fingernail nicked Morris' arm. A sensation like being tattooed all over—millions of little needles punching down into his skin—and the sound of Elise's sewing machine beats under the laughter of the women. Morris opened his eyes and saw fingernails digging into his skin, hands clutching and scratching with grips like vises. The princesses laughed and wet red threads spooled out of their mouths. Their teeth clicked together in time with the rhythm of the sewing machine. Morris tried to pull himself away but in every direction there were more hands holding him. The tiny moths were being crushed into the blood that coated him like sweat and he felt their minuscule writhings on his raw flesh. The princesses danced around him, pulling him with them, spinning and pushing him as the scents of blood and spit infused the air. Morris watched as the women tore off chunks of him and ground them up in their bright white teeth.

The sound of the sewing machine woke him. There was an added urgency in its rattle that day. In between bursts of noise, Elise cursed. Morris did not want to see her wild and angry at her machine, the needle chewing red lines into strips of fabric. He had seen enough of her agitations to know it would take little more than his presence to direct her anger toward him. He muffled his sounds as he dressed, but a moment of clumsiness sent a can of hairspray clattering to the floor loud as a grenade. Elise was in the doorway.

"What the hell are you doing?" She was in her shirt and pants from the day before. Her eyes were red and her face flushed. The unfinished dress hung from her hand like a huge snakeskin.

"Sorry. I didn't mean to." He bent to pick up the can.

"Well, can you please try to keep it down? I overslept and now this dress is so fucking late and this bitch is going to eat my head."

Morris looked up at her from the floor. The bandage on her finger was already stained with dirt and lint. He wanted to pull her down to the floor with him and just hold her. His hand closed around her wrist. She shook him free with a slight snarl.

"I don't have time for your horniness today," she said. "Sorry, babe. I'm just totally fucking stressed."

Morris remembered the lovely dark crescents formed by her eyelashes the previous night. How such simple curves could express peace and silence and how different that was from the scarlet threading of veins in her eyes now. Elise rubbed her eyes and craned her neck from side to side. Morris stood next to her and put his hands on her shoulders. He could feel the tension like a fever radiating from her. He would have to use something stronger than allergy pills.

That day he finalized the drawings, digitally adding colors and textures. He'd produced the three princesses from before, plus one with an indie-rock girl vibe: hair less Rapunzelesque, a slight ironic twist in her smile, a tiny tattoo on the wrist. They met in the conference room with representatives from the drug company that made Lunairen; two standard business guys and a lady with a bright orange scarf tucked into her charcoal grey blazer. Morris could tell from the contrast the scarf made with the dull suit that the lady would be considered the artistic one by her companions. She would be the one he made his pitch to.

Katie stood up and showed a Powerpoint that combined some of her wording with stock images of beds, pillows, night skies wrapped around crescent moons. Morris' illustrations had been added to the end of Katie's presentation. As she clicked to the next screen she stopped and swallowed hard. She glanced at the drawing and back at Morris. For the duration of the meeting he'd been trying to figure out what seemed different about her. As she stammered something Morris noticed her freckles for the first time. Had she always had them?

"Terribly sorry," she said, giving Morris a sharp look before turning back to the clients with a smile.

He glanced at the screen. What he saw there he would later be unable to explain. It was certainly his drawing style, his familiar lines and figures, but there was no way he could have made the drawing that was on the screen. The client in the orange scarf shook her head.

On the screen was Beauty's chamber, only it was Elise in the bed. Feathers drifted like autumn leaves in the room. Elise looked lovely and untroubled and peacefully dreaming, only she was being fucked by an armored prince.

"I never drew that," Morris said. "I told you we couldn't use that."

He looked at Katie for some explanation. She only wrinkled her nose and looked away. But before the clients left and Tyson gave Morris five minutes to get into his office, Morris was sure he had seen a familiar smirk on Katie's face—it was the same look the women in his dream had given him just before they tore him apart.

The ringing of his cell kept interrupting his concentration. It was work, again. Morris turned the phone off and turned back to the aisle of sleep aids. The packages on the shelf reflected the fluorescent lights overhead. All the boxes were some shade of deep blue and Morris wondered if they'd already chosen the color for the Lunairen packaging. There was a spot on Elise's wrist tattoo where the pink petal of the lotus blended into the dark outline and made a twilight shade of violet. That was the color he would pick for the box. And the name would be in the palest shade of green; the letters swooping and curling on themselves like the path of a moth in the moonlight. He bent closer to a box on the bottom shelf emblazoned with a crescent moon and tried to remember if Katie had told him that moths navigate at night by the angle of moonlight or if he had just dreamed that. Morris read the indications on the back of the box. White flowers bloomed at night so that bats could see them glow and spread their pollen. Who had told him this? The box promised a deep, restful sleep. He was sure it would be less effective than anything he could get by prescription, so he'd have to double the dose. Morris took three boxes up to the register. Tyson was probably calling again, wanting to know why Morris had never come to his office. A girl with dark shadows under her eyes and a square, masculine face bagged up the pills for him.

"Having trouble sleeping?"

"No, my girlfriend is, though. She's under a lot of stress."

The clerk shrugged as if to say that she really didn't want to know about it and handed him the bag. Morris stopped at the garbage can positioned near the door and dropped his cellphone in.

Surrounded by long shreds of fabric, tangles of thread and thick roping vines as she was, Elsie lay imprisoned in the bed. She seemed to be struggling to free herself from the clinging tendrils that engulfed her. Lashing out with her scissors, she chopped at the mass entwining her.

"Fucking mess. Stupid bullshit," she muttered. She was still in the clothes he'd seen this morning, her shirt now speckled with stray bits of red thread.

Morris stood in the doorway, holding the bag of sleeping pills behind his back.

"What's going on?" he asked. The sun had already set though it seemed impossible that so much time could have passed since he escaped the office. With a hum of electricity the streetlight outside their window flicked on, a little light tinged with gold sliding through the cracks between the blinds. Tiny white moths flitted in and out of the slatted light.

"There's no way I can finish this dress and why has your boss been calling all day? Do we have a bug problem here? I can't see where I'm supposed to be cutting. Don't just stand there all slack-jawed."

She hadn't done anything with her hair and it looked surprisingly soft and shiny, maybe longer too. All the while she spoke her scissors never stopped moving, but she made no progress in freeing herself from the web of cloth and thread.

Morris went into the kitchen and crushed four sleeping pills with a spoon right against the counter. He brushed the resulting powder into a glass and filled that with Elise's favorite drink—diet cherry soda. Careful to step around the shining steel pins on the floor, Morris brought the drink to Elise's lips, as the web had now entangled both her hands. When she looked as though she were going to berate him he tipped the glass a bit further, filling her mouth with liquid. She swallowed dutifully.

"She'll be here for the dress soon. What am I going to tell her?" Morris wiped a drop away from her bottom lip.

"I'll take care of it," he said.

"I don't feel too good."

"You're just tired baby."

"The dress isn't going to be finished."

"Just let me handle it." Morris ran his fingers through her hair, stopping to untangle the strands until his fingers slipped through.

"How? You can't."

He put his finger over her lips as though shushing a small child. Thread and hair appeared to merge into a thick cocooning mass, wrapping Elise tightly. Very soon his princess would emerge. Morris left the room so the transformation could take place.

Melancholia Canina

The hair took some getting used to. She learned to handle the itch that bloomed just under her skin as the full moon approached. Once the sun fell behind the horizon like a discarded theatre prop, her nose attuned itself to an assault of scents: household chemicals, detergent, deodorant, her own native odors underneath, meat slowly going bad despite the chill of the refrigerator. Yes. Meat. After she changed back she'd vacuum up the masses of hair and her machine would whine in protest and being fed such a quantity of fluff.

As the migraine sufferer comes to recognize the aura that precedes the pain, she came to recognize the itch in the days before her body would undergo the change. The fur sprouted all over like mushrooms after a week of rain. She expected it would itch, but each time the searing ache that enveloped her made her give an involuntary yelp. Then it was off through the window she'd remembered to leave open, under the electric beams of a full moon. Each inhaled breath crackling with signals that went right to an ancient instinctual understanding. The beats of tiny bunny hearts booming out to her like beacons.

She began to lose interest in human things. Life dulled around the edges the more time she spent as a wolf. She stopped buying bleach. Her bed was never made anymore. Full moons were her wild weekends. She went on a date—steak, as rare as you can serve it—with a man who never called back because she ate with her hands. Who needed that? He had a speck of cancer growing in his testicles anyway; she could smell it as clear as the sour tang of spoiled milk.

She was not a noble savage. Wolf nights were for the hunt and the intoxication of the night air—decay, shit, blood and fear—things that shot straight into the animal core of her, bypassing all thought. When she would wake in a pile of shed fur her deeds roiled about her like a dream half-remembered; forever slipping away from words. A sickness like hangover and a gamy taste of blood followed her back to her bedroom. She spoke less and less until she could barely remember the last thing she'd said.

The hair that she sloughed off when she shrugged out of her canine form stayed matted in the carpet. She came upon this nest of hair—much like the burrows rabbits line with fur plucked from their own delicious bellies—and tried to recall what she had once done with a machine of some kind to take the fur away. Only she was losing words like *machine* and *carpet* and had only an imprecise sense that things had once been somehow different. The chemical scents that had made her gag in the early waxing moon days were losing their strength.

She dropped onto her knees, sniffing the comforting scent of night which enveloped each strand of fur. Cold sister moon was rising again.

Lovecraft

The Florida night glowed, purple bleached to orange as the sun slipped below the horizon of strip malls and car dealerships. The air tasted of cold nights that had not yet come. This time of year, a cool draft whispered a promise that soon the long, flattening nights of heat torpor would lift. The drive to the restaurant was as clear and full of possibilities as a car ad. Lights burned with electric lucidity in vaporous yellows and blues. Little sparkling bits in the road shone like shoals of tiny fish under her headlights. Nadia pulled into a space behind the restaurant and checked her lipstick again in her rear-view mirror. She took a deep breath and practiced her smile in the mirror.

Inside, the restaurant lay underneath cobalt-blue lights, reflected as indigo puddles on each black-lacquered table. Smooth electronic music rolled like fog over the space. A thin hostess with fake green eyes asked Nadia how many would be in her party.

"Just two," she said. Then from the space to her left, a figure in black touched her elbow.

"Nadia?"

She'd found him through her computer. Calvin McLachlan, the boy she dated in high school. It had been more than ten years since she'd seen him, her last memory of him as a chubby boy who had shaved his head to play "Anarchy in The U.K." with a very amateur metal band for the school talent show. She'd imagined the same boy, older now, but with an extra sharpness to him. His grey eyes would have been refined, like muddy water turned to ice. He would tell her how the thought of her had sustained him through grim nights, how he'd never been able to shake the aura of her perfume, how he'd always hoped they would be together again. And she would betray nothing, lifting a cool cocktail to her impassive lips.

She'd dated most of the eligible men at work —men who still had a ghost of pale skin on their ring fingers. She wanted something different. Calvin used to write poems for her. Usually, they were poems about blood falling from the sky, barbed-wire growing like wheat in fields —teen angst inspired by the death metal music he adored. Still, they weren't greeting cards with glitter on them.

He was shorter than she remembered, dressed in a black suit with a black t-shirt underneath. His profile said he'd been in the Army, and he still had the haircut. Once he'd had long, dark hair. Now it was shot through with strands as grey as soapy water. He wore those technocratic eyeglasses that automatically shade the wearer from UV rays. The entire effect was blandly satanic, as though he was playing the role of an evil accountant. She smiled and he reached his arm out for a hug, which ended in a fumbled handshake. She was momentarily relieved that close contact had been averted. The girl with the fake eyes led them to a table so small, Nadia stepped on Calvin's foot a few times before she got settled.

He told her about his job, something involving computers and defense contractors. She weighed the pros and cons of the plum sake. On the one hand, it might move her into a more interesting portion of the evening; on the other, the possibility of a DUI. She ordered the sake and vegetable tempura. Sushi for him. And Kirin in the bottle. The waitress' distant smile, and then they were alone again. Nadia searched her mind for something to talk about. The sound system pumped what sounded like a hip-hop tune with breathless Japanese lyrics, a little-girl-voice floating over bass drums Nadia felt in her chest.

"So, what have you been up to? Tell me everything."

"Well, you know. English teacher. I'm working on a book in my free time."

"What about?"

The waitress appeared with a diminutive pitcher, rough-textured gunmetal grey like tarmac. She set the beer down on a glass coaster, poured the first elfin cup for Nadia, and went away. Nadia gulped down the drink, the bite in the bottom of the cup igniting a slow burn down her throat.

"It's about H.P. Lovecraft. Remember those books I used to let you borrow?"

"I don't read much," he said.

"No, when we were in school." The music seemed to have swelled in volume until the air around them vibrated. Lovecraft would have written about the *phantasmagoric thudding* or something like that, Nadia thought.

He used to wear a black t-shirt that said "Yog-Sothoth" in calculus class. That was why Nadia had noticed the boy who sat in the back corner, nearest the door. The summer before sophomore year, she'd read everything the library had by Edgar Allen Poe. In the card catalog, she found the name H.P. Lovecraft. Nadia had been reading Lovecraft's stories while she was supposed to be graphing equations. In a quickly scribbled note, she asked the new boy if he was a fan, too. Later, she found out that Yog-Sothoth was one of the dreary, aimlessly aggressive metal bands he listened to.

"Yeah, okay," he said.

"I'm writing a compendium of critical responses." She spoke in the tone she used when delivering a lecture on Charles Dickens or Emily Bronte: a little louder and more forceful than was natural. He seemed to be looking over her shoulder.

"Sounds cool," he said, as though to snip off this thread of conversation. She'd imagined a more attentive reception. She would feign reluctance while he tried to press the details of her book out of her. She imagined leaning back in her chair while he moved forward, her posture relaxed, sure of his adoration. "So, how's your job?"

"I've given up on making a difference." She laughed. He seemed confused. "You know, because they're texting in class and they couldn't give a fuck about Beowulf."

"Hey, what ever happened to Mrs. Gorewitz? You remember that time she threw me out of History class because I had headache powder in my pocket and she thought it was coke?"

"And they insisted on testing the powder?"

The waitress reappeared with their food. The sushi rolls on his plate contained a bluish, gelatinous substance that could have only been squid. *In the cursed inhabitants of Innsmouth we see again Lovecraft's preoccupation with the alien appearance of marine life,* she mentally added to her book.

Nadia attempted to lift the rice to her mouth with her chopsticks, but the grains kept tumbling away from each other.

"I heard that they tore down the old theatre," he said, dredging a roll of sushi through a puddle of soy sauce.

She chewed for a moment. The theatre was between the mall and the library; condemned for as long as she could remember. On weekends, kids with cars converged in the parking lot to play loud music and drink beer or whatever they could lift from their parents. Nadia would get one of her parents to drive her to the library so she could meet Calvin at the theatre. On school nights, they knew they only had a few hours to be together before their respective parents would be back to pick them up at the library. They'd go into the mall, leaf through all the magazines in the bookstore and buy a Mountain Dew or some Nerds to share on their walk back. Calvin tried to hold her hand the entire time, a lonely adolescent ritual. By the time she got home, Nadia's hand would smell like a penny clenched in a hot fist for too long, with a wisp of Dial soap, or whatever Calvin showered with, under the tang of metal.

"What's there now?"

"I don't know. My sister didn't say."

"That place was probably full of rats. It's amazing every kid in town didn't come down with the plague."

He laughed, perhaps a bit too loudly. The hostess with the fake eyes looked over her shoulder at them.

The local urban legend had it that the burnouts would break into the theatre to hold Black Masses and do drugs. The few times she'd been inside, all she saw was a mass of spray-painted slogans, so many layers thick that it was impossible to tell what any of them said. Most of the seats had been torn out, and the ones that remained were slashed down to the rusting metal frames.

Calvin squeezed a squid sushi roll tightly. It bulged around the black chopsticks, poised just above the soy-sauce dish. She couldn't take her eyes off the blue squid flesh hovering over the brackish sauce. She could see the slimy tentacle transposed on the mildewed tiles of the bathroom in the theatre. There was the lingering odor of dirty water, the empty space hidden from the townspeople, the possibility of entering a private world. *The abandoned town and the great ruined house are not just set pieces invoking a gothic sense of romance. In such places, the hero enters a sacred space containing the awe-inspiring horror of the chaos upon which mundane life is built.*

"Are you okay?" He made a face as though she had trailed off in mid-sentence.

"I'm fine," she said.

"Do you remember that day when we were walking past the theatre and it started to hail? It was so weird because it was August, and there weren't any clouds or anything."

She could picture the theatre, the glass over the movie posters all smashed, a scrap of faded blue paper inside, artifact of a movie that had run its course long ago. The fading yellow paint on the asphalt, veined with tough grass. She tried to imagine the hail coming down on them from a clear blue sky. Orange sun burning their black clothes to their skins with nuclear intensity.

"When was this?"

"It was in August. It must have been the summer before we started senior year. Yeah, because you were saying something about how I shouldn't cut my hair when it started coming down. I grabbed your hand and we ran under the overhang thing. It lasted a long time, too. Then you said that it wasn't hail. I picked up a piece and I was going to eat it to prove that it was ice."

Nadia drained two miniscule cups of sake in succession. The color in the restaurant wasn't blue anymore, but a tint of deep violet that made the shadows on the wall melt into the paintings of Tokyo cityscapes and black-eyed geisha on the walls. The color was like something Lovecraft would have written about; deep, indefinite and cold. She'd spent the summer before senior year on her uncle's horse ranch in New Mexico.

He put down his chopsticks and laid his hands on the table: fingernails clipped so close to the skin, she thought she could see a ridge of dried blood under one of them.

"But when I picked it up, it cut my fingers, because it wasn't ice. It was weird little chunks of glass."

"Glass?" She wondered then if she'd been mistaken. If this person just looked like Calvin, but wasn't actually him. But then, how did he know so much about her past?

"You said you knew it wasn't ice, then you put my finger in your mouth to clean the blood off."

"Calvin, I was away the whole summer."

"You must have come back early. Maybe you just forgot."

Nadia reached for the memory. She could smell the sunburnt skin, feel the heat pressing down, the scrabbling lizards darting away from their feet, but when she tried to imagine the ping of the glass ricocheting off the pavement, the feeling of his bloodied finger in her mouth, there was a neat blank space in her mind, as though cored by a hole-puncher. If she had been in a Lovecraft story, this would have been the first sign that some unknowable, alien entity was devouring her mind.

"No, it couldn't have been me." She set her cup down too hard.

"I'm positive you were there. I didn't cut my hair until after we broke up or whatever. And that day we were arguing about me wanting to cut my hair. You said right afterward that it was a sign that you were right, so I didn't cut it." He finished his beer and raised the empty bottle so the waitress would bring him another.

She'd taken *The Thing on the Doorstep* with her to New Mexico. Every night she'd looked at the sky, stars unblurred by suburban ambient glow, wondering how deep it went. The smells of hay and horse shit leaked in through the windows as she read, and now that scent came to her whenever she went back to that book. She was nowhere near the condemned theatre, she couldn't have been. It was as clear to her as the scrapes around the deadbolt on her apartment's front door, the pile of rejected outfits in the middle of her bed, the black straightening iron balanced on the edge of her sink.

"You must be thinking of someone else."

"No. I swear, it was you. You had on that damn patchouli oil that made my clothes smell like a head shop."

She would remember. If glass fell from the sky she would remember something like that. *In* The Thing on the Doorstep, *Edward Derby serves as a double of the staid narrator. Derby's own descent into madness and debauchery prefigures the narrator's fate.* Was Calvin there with someone else? She replayed the scene, and she could see her hand fitting into his, only it wasn't her hand. Her black hair plastered to a face that looked just like hers, but it wasn't hers, it was impossible that it would be hers. *It is Derby's curiosity that leaves his body open to possession by occult forces.*

"Anyway," he went on.

The bass was riding up her body from the soles of her feet, vibrating through her bones and fighting the push and pull of her veins. His mouth moved, but his words weren't reaching her. Under the deep violet color that seemed to come from cracks in the ceiling, her white rice glowed, a phosphorescent mass of tiny sea creatures. She laid the chopsticks on the table and drained the last of the sake into the cup. It was colorless and went down into her stomach like space, utterly frozen. The questions multiplied until they outnumbered the grains of rice on her rectangular plate. It seemed that in the darkness beyond their table, the waitresses and the hostess with the fake eyes were scrutinizing her.

"You were with someone else. It must have been a different person, not me."

"No. It had to be you," he said.

"Impossible." She couldn't recall him being this stubborn before.

"Look, whatever. I know what I saw. What difference does it make?"

Again, she tried to see the chunk of glass shattering on the pavement, shards scattering across the parking lot. Maybe someone else was out there, cropping up during storms of glass, living a life she was meant to have. Perhaps had she been there and lost that afternoon, the memory scraped clean out of her mind. The uncertainty loomed like the night outside, the suggestion of darkness staining the walls and ceilings of the restaurant with ink.

"It doesn't matter," he said, ending the conversation by pushing another squid roll into his mouth.

He went on talking. He even laughed at his own jokes, bits of seaweed stuck in his teeth. Army. Office politics. The waitress took away the plates and Nadia forgot to fight over the bill. Then it-was-great-seeing-you-agains and lets-do-this-again-soons. She let herself receive a hug. He smelled like beer and sea salt.

Nadia walked back to her car. The asphalt exhaled humidity. She felt the pulsing bodies of lizards concealed in the dark. In a Lovecraft story she would have needed an antique book to meet the darkness. Instead, she'd stumbled over it in a Japanese restaurant. The abyss had been inside her all along.

A waxing moon hung over the palms like an enormous eye, blind and crouched in clouds. She tried to see past the clouds, to the pinpoints of light. She could almost see them, and she envisioned rough chunks of translucent glass pummeling the sidewalk. The few stars that shone diagrammed a sullen knowledge, their slow revolving flicker a message she had no key to decode.

Violets, Covered in Snow

Spring brought a sudden burst in the population of insects. Their blurred bodies crashed against the lights in the subway station with a noise that might have been a hiss or an electrical charge. Erin stepped away from the lights, lest the ricocheting bugs rain down on her. Several were already crushed under her foot. Having found their way underground, the insects circled the only source of illumination as though it might provide a way out of this underworld. Erin checked the address of the woman again. Tereza, with a z, she'd insisted. The woman said she had no one to give the dress to, so she would welcome the little cash Erin would give her to take it away. Many women wanted to draw out the transaction with endless cups of musty tea or stale little cookies presented on a scrap of yellowed lace. They wanted Erin to know that what they were selling her was precious, important. Erin had become adept at faking interest in their sentimental tales. She would turn over an envelope with more money in it than the dress was worth and fold the garment—careful! See these pearls? Each one sewn on by the hand of a Japanese nun—into her bag. Once she returned to her apartment she laid the dress out on her dining room table. The dress was often sized for a child and its melancholy cascades of embroidery reminded her of the eyelet blouses she once wore to mass. Then she would drink a glass of water to rid her mouth of the flavor of bitter tea and circle the dress several times, admiring the tiny hand-stitched hems, the silk and linen that would have announced to the crowd the worth of the girl swathed within. With the only tool now that held her interest—a scalpel whose blade she would replace at least twice before she was done—she set to work disassembling, slicing through thread neatly and laying out the pieces so that at the end of the night the dress had been totally annihilated and lay like a butchered animal on her floor.

Erin zipped her hoodie against the bugs—beetles of some sort—pelting the tiled walls of the station. The insects gave off a faint plum-black iridescence where the sodium lights caressed them. The rhythm of the train on the tracks throbbed under the crackle of exoskeleton against glass. Erin boarded the train and checked the time on her phone—an overcomplicated piece of technology that Logan had insisted on buying her. She still had his last text message saved on the device. Now that Logan was gone she rarely used the thing except to see what time it was. A man on the train coughed into his tweed sleeve. He wore beat-up canvas sneakers. Erin imagined he thought this the sartorial equivalent of a shrug, a way to undercut the seriousness of a tweed coat. Maybe he just couldn't afford new shoes. Logan had worn nice shoes. His wife brought a few pairs back from Argentina for him when she went to visit her family. Erin pictured Logan's wife opening her suitcase with a flourish; lifting out a pair of shoes and presenting them to him as a sort of reverse Cinderella. How much nicer it would have been for her imagination to make her a wicked stepmother, tossing the shiny leather shoes down on the floor and making him stoop to retrieve them. But she had no reason to believe this image. The man with the sneakers lurched forward slightly as the train pulled away from the station. Erin, seized with the fear that every little detail she noticed from this point forward would only point back to Logan, bit her thumb as a charm to ward off the thought.

She was the little seamstress. At least, that's what she imagined Logan had told his wife. She'd met him over the cuffs of his suit trousers. A faint odor of sweet tea haloed his clothes. He drank it constantly, laden with condensed milk and sugar. His wife had some sort of job involving marketing and made more money than he did. Erin listened to all this as she knelt by Logan's feet, carefully sliding pins into the hems of his pants.

His first kiss, when it came, tasted of sweet cream with bitter black tannin underneath. He'd come into her shop late one evening. She was just about to close, she explained. But he really needed her help, he said. This suit, it was for an important event. Erin's heart hammered in her chest as she turned the sign to *Closed*. Alone in her shop with the handsome client, Erin laughed at his charming talk, attempting to put them both at ease. Not in a thousand universes would she have expected him to take hold of her hand the way he did when she handed the finished pants back to him. She should have pulled back then, but she didn't. His hand on hers was surprisingly soft. Headless cloth bodies stood guard over Logan and Erin in those moments as they drew closer. Erin tumbled down into the kiss that came next like a rabbit caught in a snare.

Much later, after they'd snuck into her workroom to have sex one afternoon, he confessed that the suit he'd brought her that day had been a ruse to spend some time with her. Erin's throat burned with unreleased tears. No one had ever gone so far just to be in her presence.

She hoped the old woman tonight would not try to keep her too long with tea and sad old tales. She wanted to be back in her apartment with only the scintillating whisper of silk falling away from her cutting table. She told the women she restored the dresses. In a way, that was true. She restored them to the scraps of fabric they had originated from.

Erin bit her thumb. Her mother's voice admonished her once again: *and I suppose he's the first married man ever to feel that way.* Logan's specialty was the work of Franz Kafka. He sent her emails in which he wrote of his *proscribed longing* to be with her. Into her ear he whispered that he knew he shouldn't but it had just been so long since he'd had a connection like this. From anyone else, this would have sounded fake, but the tremor in his voice and the way his hand gripped hers—as if she were the only thing anchoring him to this world—convinced her. Recalling the thrilling sensation of Logan's hand on the back of her neck, Erin's teeth sunk deeper into the meat of her thumb. The man in the sneakers looked over his newspaper at her, brow furrowed. She shot him a bird and he looked away. When the train stopped at her station, the man in sneakers stood far back to let her pass.

At the door to the old woman's apartment, she hesitated for a moment. On the other side of the door waited the velvet seats where arms had worn the nap off the fabric, the lace curtains yellowed and stiff with dust.

"Are you here for the dress?" the woman who opened the door asked. Her hair was much longer than Erin expected, done in a crown of cinereal braids. Erin nodded and the woman motioned for her to come into the apartment.

The interior was dark and smelled of loam and leaves. As Erin's eyes adjusted to the darkness she was able to pick out dozens of terrariums scattered around the room.

"Sit," the woman said.

Erin dropped onto a couch, bringing herself face to face with a caterpillar wending its way across a twig in one of the terrariums.

"Are these butterflies?"

"Moths." The woman passed a china teacup into Erin's hand.

"They can't live long, can they? I mean, in here."

"Perhaps not, but they have a beautiful life."

Erin took a sip of the tea. It had a hint of ginger which she hadn't expected. The spice burned her sinuses and added it own earthy scent to the sylvan odor in the room. A moth in the tank just behind Erin fluttered against the screen lid, making a machine-gun beat with its silvery wings.

"The light," the woman said, gesturing to the ceiling. "That one is trying to fly to the light. You must have lived in the city your whole life. Have you seen insects before?" She raised a sugar-coated cookie to her mouth and scissored tea-stained teeth through it.

"I guess I've never paid attention to them."

The woman set the bitten cookie—now resembling a broken and snow-dusted rock—back on the serving plate. She held the plate out to Erin.

"Don't be afraid, a little extra meat might make you look more womanly."

Erin hated that word—*womanly*—with its inherent judgment. It was one of the few complementary words Logan had used for his wife. She associated it with the sort of women who could wear short white skirts over long tan legs, dispensing air kisses over the charming xylophone of metal bangles.

"Oh, no, really." The cookies looked even less appealing than ever now that she could see the hard beige and sandstone-like interior. Erin bit her thumb instead. It was beginning to go numb and shade to purple from her teeth's repeated assaults.

"I have more than twenty-five varieties here, all raised from cocoons. I used to go around the world with my husband gathering them. Now I get them mailed to me. Imagine that. I spent three days on a mountain in China searching every twig for a single cocoon, and now they drop them in the mail like postcards. Would you believe it?"

"Hmm."

"My son, he tells me always to get a dog or a cat. I tell him we raised moths for years before you were born. We always had cocoons; I don't want to stop now. He thinks I go mad with just these to talk to." She lifted the lid from one of the tanks and reached her finger inside. A dusty creature with feathery antennae clung to her hand, slowly flapping its wings. She gave a shake and the moth fluttered back into the tank.

Erin peered into the darkness of the tank. The moth's wings folded over its body reflected the available light like raw silk. A crocheted doily stained with dirty water under the aquarium echoed the downy shades of the moth's wing. Beside the tank was a framed photo of a young boy holding a rabbit. He smiled anxiously into the camera, his hand tense across the back of the rabbit's neck as though he were holding something unbearably hot.

"Ah. My son." Tereza smiled and angled the frame toward Erin. "He must be about your age now. A professor."

A sensation like her heart being thrown down a flight of stairs nearly brought Erin down. She knew intimately that intent sadness in the boy's eyes. A professor. She barely got out her next question, and when the woman replied that his name was Logan, Erin had to find a place for the china teacup as fast as her trembling hands would allow.

"Sit, please."

Erin let herself be maneuvered into a chair. Had Logan ever mentioned his mother's name? Had he said something about moths that she hadn't been paying attention to, so fixed was she on parsing every scrap of information about his marriage?

"You must be hungry. Eat a little something, at least."

She waved away the stony cookies.

"Oh, I'm sorry. Are you unwell?"

"No. I'm fine."

The woman set the plate down on one of the tanks with the zing of ceramic on metal. She smoothed her crown of braids.

"I have a good brandy, too, if you need." She didn't wait for a response and was pressing a small cut crystal glass into Erin's hand. "I hope there isn't something upsetting," she said, nodding as Erin swallowed down the drink.

"No. Just. He really looks like someone I know."

"My Logan?"

"It's a coincidence." She grasped for any indication this was a dream. A spring from the very real and solid chair was poking her ass. The beat of the moth's wings behind their dark glass sounded almost like the marching of very tiny feet from far, far off. Erin swallowed, the warmly perfumed burn of liquor still on her tongue. What had the woman just said? *My Logan.* My Logan. Nobody's Logan.

"I hope that doesn't distress you," Tereza said.

"What?" Erin looked down at her thumb, its violet flush reminder enough that thoughts of him still commanded her mind. "It was just unexpected, that's all." She hoped she sounded casual enough to divert any further questions.

"Your tea is going cold. Let me get you a fresh cup."

Women had attempted to keep Erin from leaving before. She had been told that she was the first person to visit in months; that she looked just like a dead sister; that there was a nephew—a dentist—who would be just perfect for her. But the regard of this woman—Logan's mother, after all—as she took the tea cup away made Erin want to smooth over her little display of emotion as quickly as possible. She wasn't here to cozy up to her ex-lover's mother. She wanted the dress. Only the dress, she told herself.

While Tereza worked in the kitchen Erin glanced around the room to see if there were any pictures of Logan's wife. She never knew her real name, only that people called her Lola, which had struck Erin as the sort of name engineered by a woman who wanted to seem carefree and fun-loving and hid the sharpness of a pin under her smiles. Dietrich's character in *The Blue Angel* was a Lola. Logan had described her as exacting and practical. She belonged to social clubs. She had a huge family in South America that had taken her on skiing excursions when she was a girl. She wore an emerald ring that had been given to her by some long-ago admirer and thought it was funny that Logan opposed this.

And what did Erin have? She thought of the magazines pushed under the bed when she had first brought Logan to her apartment. Her tiny dressmaker's shop hung with drawings she'd done when once upon a time she'd thought of becoming a fashion designer. Her clunky shoes that had caused a little girl to exclaim to her mother that a man must be in the ladies' room. Her shoes. Man shoes. When she'd ask Logan what interest he could have in her, he chuckled indulgently as though at a child. He said he wanted her, *needed* her, even. But Erin marked that he had no real answer. There were words enough to describe his desire to sleep with her, but no reason why it was Erin and not any other woman. Logan recited litanies of his wife's neglect as though they proved his love for Erin. He and Lola went to charity balls while Erin slept with the cellphone on the pillow next to hers—in case Logan stole away long enough to call her—like a Cinderella forgotten by her fairy godmother.

"So, why moths?" she asked when Tereza returned with the teacup. Erin steered her away from the subject of her emotional reaction.

"I have always found them fascinating. They are like the night-cousins of butterflies. The tender little cocoons that give us silk. Not all of them will fly into a flame, you know. Because they're nocturnal they use the light of the moon to navigate the darkness." She sat across from Erin and smoothed her black dress over her knees.

"Do you get silk from them?"

"Not all cocoons can be used that way. Many thousands of cocoons have to be gathered first. They usually boil them with the pupae inside." She picked up the half-eaten cookie she had left on the plate and took a bite.

"That's horrible."

"It's the silk, not the silkworm that people want. You must make use of silk in your work?" She brushed a few stray crumbs off her chin.

Erin wondered how many silkworms it took to make even a yard of the silks she had in her shop. The thought of all the pupae wrapped tight in their cocoons, expecting to emerge with wings into the perfumed night being dumped into a cauldron of boiling water seemed especially cruel to her. She was usually indifferent to other people's pain. She couldn't afford to care about other lonely souls when she was barely keeping herself afloat.

"But you must be wanting to see the dress," Tereza said, standing and returning a crescent of cookie to the plate. She disappeared into another room, leaving Erin to wonder how she had come to be in this damp apartment. Surely she had contacted this woman. Or had she been contacted? It was known among women who fortune or time had left daughterless that there was a little seamstress who would buy your precious wedding dress at a good price. Hadn't it been this woman who had called her shop offering the dress for much less than she normally paid? The picture of young Logan holding the rabbit stared back at her with a hint of menace where she had once seen unease. His hand appeared to be on the verge of squeezing the rabbit too tight. Perhaps the camera had caught him in the moment before his youthful clumsiness had snapped the poor thing's neck.

Erin looked again for a photo that might be of Lola. She examined the pictures over several of the tanks, her heart pounding. She feared what it would be like to know finally what the wife of the man she still loved looked like. In her imaginings, Lola had no face. She always spoke with her back turned or with hair the color of Tereza's brandy veiling her face.

"Here it is," Tereza announced, laying out a large box shedding parcel paper.

Erin turned away from the pictures and approached the box. This moment was usually crucial if she were going to get what she came for. She didn't want another show of emotion to scare the seller off. But now the dress seemed like part of a trap. It could be possible that she was in this apartment because someone wanted her there. Tereza stood back. Erin carefully reached for the lid, conscious now that the woman might be scrutinizing her on behalf of her son or the occult Lola. Inside the box lay a dress with the finest silk detailing on the bodice. Tiny petals of silk organza overlapped one another like scales in subtle shades of ivory and gold. They shimmered in the dreary electric light as though woven from fine threads of sunlit spiderweb. Erin drew her hand back. The dress had come out of the most fantastic tale. To touch it would surely destroy it.

"Yes, you like it?"

"Where did it come from?" She had seen hand-stitches that made ribbons appear to float away from the dress, embroidery worked with glass beads so small they barely accommodated a hole in the center, but never anything as unique as this.

"Very special and rare, this one. The dressmaker did only one or two of these a year. It took her that long, too, to finish the dress. If you ate too much and grew fat before then, well, your tears were all your own. The dressmaker could not go back and let it out." She lifted the dress out of the box. A cascade of eggshell silk scaled all over with fine petals went down to the hem. Erin wondered if Lola had seen this dress. She wouldn't have recognized its beauty, or the hours of labor that must have gone into it. Erin imagined that Lola would have dismissed it as an old-fashioned frock. The dress was scented with dust and violets and some long-gone June afternoon. Erin could just picture the woman, Tereza, as the radiant blonde girl who had worn this dress, those grey braids once aureate coils from a Botticelli painting, the warm sun gilding her eyelashes and moistening her palms."

"All sewn by hand?"

"Oh yes, and just the dressmaker would see it. The family would bring the girl to her. She was an old woman by the time I came but with great long streaks of black in her hair yet. She had no family of her own, and some said one or both of her parents had been a gypsy. She used her hands to measure you, like this," the woman moved her hands over Erin's arm, rotating at the thumb to move further up. Her cold fingers reminded Erin of the way Logan used to envelop both her hands in his to warm them in the winter. "She kept it all in her head. It was said that she could see a girl's future. She made the dress in secret, and the first time the girl saw it was the night before the wedding. Could you believe that it always fit perfectly?"

The seamstress must have had a fantastic memory to keep the girl's dimensions in her mind like that. Darts, tucks, curves cut too shallow could all make the dress a misshapen sack. Her own struggles with fitting demanding clients had taught Erin that a spare fragment of an inch here or there could ruin a garment completely. She pictured the seamstress in a storybook cottage, measuring out spans of satin by the hand-length. Surely, that was talent akin to witchcraft.

"And she made this one for you? Has anyone else ever worn it?" Erin ran the tips of her fingers over the organza petals. By the end of the night they could be scattered across her apartment floor like cherry blossoms fallen from the boughs.

"Yes, made for me. Who else would have worn it?"

"Well, I wasn't sure. A daughter?" Or Lola. Erin wasn't ready to believe that there might not be some ulterior motive here. Perhaps Tereza had learned of Logan's infidelity on her own and resolved to see this other woman.

"No, I just have a son." The woman stepped away from the dress to peek into one of the moth tanks. Erin looked for the ends of the seams, where she usually began her dissections.

Snip the thread down the seam and pull away the pieces like peeling back a dead thing's skin. These dresses were often the last remaining wisps of a ghostly seamstress' work, and in undoing them Erin knew she was taking something rare and unique away from the world. Perhaps that was the source of the relief she felt once the dress was disassembled and lying with the mysteries of its construction stripped away. Then the urge to undo all this singular beauty abated and Erin felt a reprieve had temporarily been granted her.

"And you're sure you want to sell it?" It was by far the most exquisite dress Erin had ever seen. To take it apart would take hours of fine work. While seeking out white threads to cut her mind blocked out the dead promises Logan had whispered into the phone at night; the smug purse of her mother's mouth as she poured another glass of wine and said *They always say they want to leave their wives*; the hairbrush wound with what must have been Lola's brown hair in his bag next to ungraded papers.

"I have no one to leave it to. My Jurgen is gone many years now and I am getting old. I will even have to stop getting cocoons in the mail soon." She turned away from the moths in their glass enclosures and smoothed her silver braids.

"Yes, but you might have a granddaughter someday? Why not give it to her?" Erin feared her questions might lead the woman to take back the dress, but she couldn't resist this opportunity to learn more about Logan's marriage. Though she suspected this line of questioning would lead her to more tears and sleepless nights, a thrill ran through her that her questions at least would be answered.

"I want someone who will appreciate it," she put her hand on Erin's arm again, the cold fingers as light as hollow bones.

What she wanted to do with the dress, if seen from outside, would likely seem as heartless as harvesting the silk from the sleeping worm. Erin wanted to tell her then that the dress would be pulled apart slowly like the boiling water disintegrating the silkworm's cocoon. See if Tereza would still think she wanted to preserve this sorceress-made dress. Tereza squeezed Erin's arm and smiled.

"Sit, let me tell you the rest of the story."

Erin sat, but her gaze lingered on the dress like a hungry dog before warm bloody meat. If she could just start cutting the threads, she could soothe herself. Her thumb throbbed with pain and she pressed it hard with the nail of the other thumb to bring the pain into sharper relief.

"When I went up to the old woman's house it was January. My papa had given the money for the dress in an envelope with a red ribbon on it, and I was to take it to the woman on my own. It was so cold, and the woman's little house had just a small fire. She looked into the parcel and said there was not enough. Now, my papa was ill, and he'd worked very hard to get this bit of coin together. I was the only daughter, you see, and my mother had died when I was just a little one. Papa wanted to make me the most beautiful bride in the village that summer."

The woman went to the kitchen and poured a measure of brandy into her tea.

"You want more?"

Erin waved away the bottle.

"As I said, I had come in the snow very far to give this seamstress the money, and she tells me there isn't enough. I was still young and foolish then so I began to cry, thinking the woman would take pity on me. Well, the old woman clapped her hands and commanded me to stop like I was a little barking dog. Could you believe that?"

Erin knew the question was purely rhetorical and kept her silence. She had believed many things—that Logan loved her as he said, that he would leave his wife to be with her—and was not much in the mood for believing anymore.

"The old woman tells me that tears make no coins, so if I wanted the dress I would have to bring something else to her. I asked what she wanted. She tells me to bring her a bunch of violets. But there are no violets in January, I say. The old woman says that now this is the only payment she will take for the dress. I had heard from other girls who had been completely refused by the woman and I was afraid she would refuse me too.

What could I do? Off into the forest I went, though I had no hope of finding what she demanded."

Behind her, a moth fluttered it wings, creating a tendril of updraft that Erin felt floating a few hairs up. The hairs on her neck and arms stood in response, a phantasmal shiver breaking over her skin like a wave. As Tereza talked, Erin imagined she could see something of Logan's expression in the way she tilted her head. She seemed to be pausing to listen to an imperceptible sound—a moth's distressed flutter or the creaking of a cocoon opening.

"I walked deeper and deeper into the forest. I could not go back now and tell my papa that the old woman would not make the dress when he was sick. It was bitter cold. Soon the skies dropped down snow so thick I could barely see my hand before my face. I came into a clearing in the trees and the snow lessened until I could see a man sitting by a fire. Why did you come here, dear little girl? he asked. I told him I was searching for violets. He was older than me, but not yet an old man, with very handsome reddish hair. This is no time for violets, when all is covered with snow, he said. I sat down then on a log near the fire and began to cry again, this time because I knew for sure that my papa would die before he would see me wed in the summer. The man pulled a brand from the fire and took my hand, leading me off into the forest. There, he waved the flaming branch under a tree telling me all the while to calm my crying. The snow melted away and there were bright violets there underneath, thick as a rug. I fell to my knees and snatched them up quick. The man stroked my hair and wiped a tear from my cheek. Now run along, but tell no one where you've found these, he told me."

She emptied the teacup and set it with a satisfied clatter back on the saucer.

"And? Obviously, she made the dress."

"Yes, but she was not happy to see me. She grumbled that I was favored, but not always. She told me that I would not trip through life untouched, but that could be said of all of us. I went home and only saw her again when the dress was ready. When first I put it on, a stray needle stuck me and the mother of my groom said there would now be a misfortune. I didn't heed that pinprick until a few years later when my groom died."

These were the moments Erin tried to avoid. Tereza fell silent and closed her eyes a moment, blinking back a bad memory. Loss and loneliness. It fit Erin so right, so close to her skin; her only companion. She felt that under a thin armor of frost she soaked up pain like a sponge, and her own sadness had already filled her to capacity. All these women she'd visited with knew what it was to lose someone.

"I'm sorry," Erin said.

"Well, some years later I met my Jurgen and married again, but I did not wear the dress. Some of the girls of my town whispered that the old woman had sewn a curse into it."

"But later you were happier, right?"

"Yes, of course, but I was different then."

The ethereal beauty of the dress masked a tragic secret. She wondered what would happen if she wore the dress. It might leave its imprint on her as well, as a tight garment impresses its seams and folds into the flesh so that they're still visible on the naked body for an hour later. And perhaps she'd lose the man she loved as well, only in a more complete way that would take him further than the limbo in which she lived now; knowing that Logan was shopping or eating breakfast with loveless Lola, the jail warden of Erin's happiness.

When Erin slipped into bed the feeling of Logan's legs brushing against hers under the sheets haunted her. On those rare nights when he'd been able to stay with her all night she felt his breath against her cheek and felt as though they were sewn together into one skin, one blood. As they sat together in a café near her shop sharing a jalousie one afternoon, she realized the distant, dreamy look in his eyes gave him a melancholy appearance that made her want to hold this sharp world far away from him. She seized his wrist then, hoping to convey comfort to him, a silent promise that she was with him. His wan smile in response strengthened the bitter sweetness of the moment, her hand wrapped around the wrist of a man who should not have been there with her. She was likely projecting her own vulnerabilities onto him in that moment, she was now aware. There had been other men in her life, but they mostly wanted to *Keep it casual* and didn't see the need to *define things*. None of those men would have ever used the word *longing* in connection with her. Erin still didn't know what had made Logan choose her. Maybe she'd just been convenient; a needy woman for a man who wanted to be needed.

Still, when Logan's last words reached Erin through the phone, she felt a piece of herself being torn away, as the sections of dress she worked on came unstitched, irrevocably, one from the next. He said he'd made a mistake and that it was over, as if their love was just a story he'd dreamt up and now he could declare it was ended. As if that would just make her stop loving. When she asked if it was because his wife had found out, he just hung up the phone. Erin held the hot piece of plastic and glass that had once carried the voice of her beloved to her ear until the thing impatiently beeped to alert her to the dead connection.

In the picture, young Logan stood frozen in innocence. If she took Logan away from Lola she would take him from Tereza too, leaving her with her silent moths and the stony cookies and time ticking down her days.

"Is the dress cursed?"

"What do I know of such things?" Tereza laughed, a hint of unease under her smile. "We think many things when we are young and unwise."

In the darkness of her bedroom Logan had held Erin's hand and sworn he would be with her forever.

"Do you think I could try it?"

Tereza leaned away, surprised at the request.

"Well, if you really wish to."

"I do." Erin laughed to herself a little to say this phrase. "I don't believe in curses. Besides, even if it is true, I have no one to love anyway."

Tereza picked up the dress and helped Erin undo the long

trail of buttons going up the back. Erin's shoes thudded onto the floor, followed by her jeans and her hoodie. She raised her foot to step into the dress. She expected a torrent of guilt to follow her into the dress, but her legs met the silk with the smoothness of slipping into warm water. As Tereza reached for the first button Erin considered what might happen to Logan as she proceeded. He might have an accident in the subway, or his electric teapot might malfunction and burn down his office with him inside. Lola would wear a tight black dress and no stockings to his funeral. Even in March, her legs would have the bronze sheen of a Brazilian beauty queen. Tereza might sit next to her—or not—at the funeral, a grim curve to her mouth suggesting she had done this many times over.

The buttons slipped into their loops all the way up Erin's back. The dress was a smidge tight in the waist, just enough that Erin felt the resistance of the fabric if she exhaled deeply, but otherwise it fit her quite well. The petals glowed in shades of gold, copper and rose as Erin moved toward the light. Tereza took a step away and clasped her hands together.

"Oh, you look lovely. Come see in the mirror."

Erin followed her into the bedroom. In keeping with the rest of the apartment, the bedroom had moth hatching tanks atop every vertical surface. A long mirror with a triangular chunk missing from the bottom showed Erin her reflection. The tiny organza petals all over the dress made it look like she was covered with fluttering moths. The skin across her cheekbones flushed pink and her lank black hair flared raven blue against the scintillating shades that played across the dress. She couldn't remember the last time she looked so good. Her reflection in the darkened glass of the subway car earlier that night had shown her a woman with purple half-moons under her eyes, dry flaking lips and a red nose. Now she looked radiant and whole. Sorcery indeed. Who could resist her in such a dress?

She turned to see herself from the back and as she twisted a pain stung her hip. She clutched the spot. Tereza was at her side, helping her pull the needle free from the dress. Erin held it between her fingers. The narrow pin, blackened with age, spilled a dot of blood onto the silk of the dress.

"Oh dear, let me get you a tissue," Tereza said.

The droplet formed a starburst as the fabric of the dress drank it in. Logan would probably be preparing to go to dinner with Lola now. As Tereza fetched a tissue, Erin wondered how long it would take for Logan to finally be erased from her mind. One day very soon she would walk all the way to her shop without once recalling the pressure of his hand on hers. A deep, comforting black sleep would descend on her at night and no tears would touch her pillow. Her thumb would be bruised and sore no longer. Erin remembered that Cinderella's sisters had cut their toes off in an attempt to win the prince. All she'd had to give up was a single drop of blood.

"Thank you," Erin said, pressing the tissue to the spot where the pin had pricked her.

A moth beat its wings against the metal mesh covering its tank. Erin imagined throwing open the windows and letting all the moths escape, off into a night where they would be free as she would be too, free of love's tight zipped hold. Wings fluttered in anticipation.

Once Upon A Time: The Uses of the Fairy Tale

The fairy tale reaches back to an oral tradition of tales believed to be passed from woman to woman. In these stories, violence collides with the fantastic. Considered a child's form, fairy tales have been used to convey warnings, moral lessons, or as violent entertainment. Bruno Bettelheim, in *The Uses of Enchantment*, defines character in the fairy tale as "essentially one-dimensional, enabling the child to comprehend its actions and reactions easily" (p74). Bettelheim focused on the child as the fairy tale's intended audience because he saw dark and sometimes frightening content of these tales as necessary stepping stones in psychic development. The fairy tale presents readers with easily recognizable characters and fantastical events that border on the *grotesque* as defined by Morner and Rausch in *From Absurd to Zeitgeist*: "characterized by exaggeration and distortion of the natural or the expected" (p93). The violence and reductive simplicity of the fairy tale creates a reality that is both removed and yet distilled from mundane life. The characters that populate these tales—evil stepmothers, virtuous orphans, handsome princes—are established figures in literature. Bettelheim described the psychological need for fairy tales as follows:

The juxtaposition of opposite characters is not for the purpose of stressing right behavior as would be true for cautionary tales . . . Presenting the polarities of character permits the child to comprehend easily the difference between the two, which he could not do as readily were the figures drawn more true to life, with all the complexities that characterize real people. (p9)

If psychological complexity is sacrificed for familiarity in the fairy tale, then thematic and archetypal concerns often step in to carry the weight of the story. While the figures may be recognizable—the witch, the child, the protector—the surrounding elements of the story are freighted with potential meaning. I think it's no accident that so many fairy tales mine the same primal ground; blood, night, forest and fear.

My own interest in fairy tale motifs stems in part from an early introduction to the subversively feminist fairy tales of Angela Carter's *The Bloody Chamber*. In this book—one I evangelize for at every opportunity—an ancient vampire meets her doom in the form of a rational young Englishman. Red Riding Hood welcomes her date with the wolf. A Beauty releases her own inner Beast. I'm drawn to utilize the elements of fairy tale in my own fiction because the form combines that archetypal familiarity with the strangeness of magical events and characters. This hybridization of the real with the imaginary allows me to explore how my characters react to the unknown. I strive to tell stories that take place in a rarefied world that is only possible when the magical collides with the mundane. In the fairy tale, the drama often involves extreme acts: poisonings, resurrections, transformations that appear less credible against a backdrop that does not employ the aesthetics of the grotesque. Here I intend to give some concrete examples of the effects that can be achieved with fairy tale themes. What follows is a discussion of three authors and their use of fairy tale elements in fiction. Alice Munro, William Trevor and Margaret Atwood are masters of the short story form. The differing ways each uses the fairy tale mirrors the range of functions fairy tales have been assigned by our culture.

Alice Munroe's "Royal Beatings," one of her series of tales about young Rose and her stepmother Flo, takes its title from the cathartic violent discipline Rose intends to provoke from her father. Rose and Flo are confined to the house together; Rose baits Flo with her misbehavior in between absorbing Flo's grim cautionary tales. Against the realistic backdrop of a mixed household, Rose plays the role of orphaned heroine, while Flo stands in for the wicked stepmother. Unlike a true fairy tale, however, Munro makes these roles explicit. The characters are aware of how they fit together: which role each is to is to take on in order to enact the tale. This drama is confined to the domestic, and the principal players are the daughter and her stepmother. Munro's placement of the conflict within the domestic sphere sets up parallel themes with such fairy tales as "Cinderella" or "Snow White." Rose's brother is "not committed to the household struggle" (p129). Rose's father is "tired in advance, maybe, on the verge of rejecting the roles he has to play" (p131-132). Rose is aware that the course of events is predetermined. Of her father, she observes:

> *He is like a bad actor, who turns a part grotesque. . .That is not to say he is pretending, that he is acting, and does not mean it. He is acting, and he means it. Rose knows that. . .* (p133)

By outlining the contours of these archetypal figures, Munro highlights the ways in which her characters break out of their roles. Despite her identification with the Cinderella role, Rose does not embody all the qualities of the heroine her story hints at. Flo is the one scrubbing the floor on her hands and knees, not Rose. Unlike Snow White's stepmother, Flo appears to have no overt lust for power, but claims that "it was for Rose she sacrificed her life" (p130). Flo's powerlessness is illustrated when the washrag she throws at Rose's face "falls against Rose's leg and she raises her foot and catches it, swinging it negligently against her ankle" (p130). Flo must make Rose's father ("king of the royal beatings" (p117)) commit the act of violence, as she doesn't possess the strength to do it. Munro evokes the wicked stepmother role here, yet she exposes an understanding of the helplessness that frustrates Flo into the final act of violence, the titular "Royal Beating."

In invoking the fairy tale in "Royal Beatings," Munro focuses on the violence contained within the form and discards the virtue associated with moralizing versions of fairy tales. The tale—Flo's explanation of what happened to town oddity, the dwarf Becky Tyde—within the story mirrors the structure and theme of the fairy tale. According to town gossip, Flo explains, Becky's father was savagely beaten, perhaps in retaliation for an act of incest. Munro highlights the aspects of the fairy tale she utilizes in the following passage:

Rose could be drawn back—from watching the wind shiver along the old torn awning, catch in the tear—by this tone of regret, caution, in Flo's voice. Flo telling a story—and this was not the only one, or even the most lurid one, she knew—would incline her head and let her face go soft and thoughtful, tantalizing, warning. (123-124)

Rose sees such stories as warnings, which fairy tales can often be. The tale that Flo tells is devoid of any real moral lesson, and Munro's telling words "tantalizing" and "lurid" get to the true fascination of the tale for both Flo and Rose: the enchanting violence that such a spectacle provides. The fascination of violence appears in Rose's fantasy of a royal beating, which Munro describes as "an occasion both savage and splendid" (p117). The tale within "Royal Beatings" draws parallels between Becky Tyde and Rose as skewed versions of the orphaned fairy tale heroine. The violence in Becky Tyde's story does nothing to transform her. She cannot be changed from beast into beauty, despite the ritual of violence done on her behalf. Rose cannot fit Becky into the roles assigned to her in Flo's story: "the butcher's prisoner, the cripple daughter, a white streak at the window; mute, beaten, impregnated" (p124). The Becky she meets in her parents' grocery store is an "oddity and public pet, harmless and malicious," (p124) divorcing her from the virtuous role of the fairy tale heroine. Likewise, Rose is not the clear-cut victim of her own tale of violence. The word "corruption" enters Munro's description of Rose, (p130, p136) her need to provoke the beating sets the action of the entire story. During the violence, she "plays [her father's] victim with a self-indulgence that arouses, and maybe hopes to arouse, his final, sickened contempt." (p134) As in the Becky Tyde story, Rose's tale comes to no moral conclusion. Flo grows old, but remains "crafty and disagreeable" (p138). Rose sends Flo away, but cannot exorcise the fascination with violence that links them.

The work of Angela Carter inspired my short story "Beauty Asleep," an exploration of what happens when a story a fairy tale takes on a life of its own. The remade fairy tales of Carter's *The Bloody Chamber* reveal the dark implications haunting the subtexts of these stories. As in Munro's tales of domesticity and violence, a thread of Gothic menace runs through Carter's stories. In "The Company of Wolves," Carter re-examines the story of Little Red Riding Hood from many perspectives in order to tease out the hidden messages of the tale. Carter's narrative remains abstracted from her characters in order to demonstrate the sexual subtext of this tale in which a young girl is tempted by a wild beast to succumb to the pleasures of the flesh. My story shares Carter's concern with how fairy tales set gender expectations. The rescuing prince and victimized princess are present in my story as ideas that take a more sinister turn in the protagonist's mind. My protagonist's increasing need to escape into the fantasy world of the fairy tale leads him to take ever more extreme measures to make reality conform to his fantasy. His obsession with the liminal state of sleep and the intrusion of dream-like imagery into his mind illustrates his engulfment by the nebulous realms of his fantasy. Morris, an artist alienated from his girlfriend, becomes engrossed in enacting his own version of the "Sleeping Beauty" story. As he works on a campaign for a sleeping pill, the fairytale imagery of his art exerts its influence over his relationship. He intends to transform his girlfriend into the princess in the story by keeping her asleep, and is willing to go to dark extremes to accomplish this.

The subtext of the "Sleeping Beauty" story is introduced through Katie, one of Morris' co-workers, when she recounts the original conclusion of the story. Of the prince who is supposed to awaken Beauty from her enchanted sleep, Katie says:

Well, he makes his way into the tower and all that, only he does a lot more to the princess than just kiss her. He fucks her and prances off on his merry way. Only later after she has a pair of baby Prince

Juniors one of them sucks the magical splinter out of her finger and that's what wakes her up.

It's the introduction of this image of rape that plants the seed of obsession in Morris' mind. The implication of violence is carried throughout the story and surfaces in Morris' presentation of a drawing of the rape taking place to the clients that have hired him to design advertisements for a sleeping pill. Morris' girlfriend Elise is hardly the passive Beauty he requires to act out the story, thus he finds it necessary to subdue her by rendering her unconscious. The story Morris enacts is a grotesque inversion of "Sleeping Beauty" in which Morris both accepts and distances himself from the role of Prince. Morris resists identification with the Prince-as-rapist in his conversation with Katie. Rather than taking up the charge to awaken Beauty from her sleep, Morris finds the only way to fulfill the fantasy is to create a Sleeping Beauty out of Elise. As Morris takes steps to enact the Sleeping Beauty tale, he becomes more monster than prince.

William Trevor's "In at the Birth," in which an elderly woman, Miss Efoss, is hired to watch a neighbor's child— with an injunction never to enter the room in which the child sleeps— follows a fairy tale formula. The story opens with the familiar phrase "once upon a time" (p102), suggesting the action takes place far in the remote past, though the story is filled with details of the modern world. Trevor uses the fairy tale structure to focus on the cycle of life. As in a fairy tale, the reader is given a brief expository explanation of the protagonist's background. Children are a strong theme in this story. The loss of Miss Efoss's child is given in unsentimental language: "Miss Efoss's baby died during a sharp attack of pneumonia; and shortly afterward, the child's father packed a suitcase one night" (p102). Here Trevor reduces his characters to simplified roles. Childlessness is a motivation in several fairy tales and Trevor plays with the reader's expectations in this story. Miss Efoss discovers that the "child" that she has been caring for is in fact an elderly man, quite likely her predecessor. It is not

Miss Efoss, the childless woman, who goes to great lengths to have a child. Her experience affords her no special status in the modern world. Though Mr. Dutt calls her "a wise woman," (p110) Miss Efoss does not play the role of the knowledgeable elder in Trevor's world. The circular movement of the story returns Miss Efoss to an infantile state. Miss Efoss's return to the childless Dutts fulfills their desire for a child in a way that mirrors the magical children born of wishing that populate fairy tales such as "Snow White." The narrative distance between Trevor's authorial voice and his protagonist reinforces this fairy tale structure. Trevor preserves a detached narrative voice when he describes Miss Efoss's return to the Dutts: "Her flat became bare and cheerless. In the end there was nothing left except the property of the landlord" (p112). This distance allows the true motives of the characters to remain shaded. Plot takes precedence over psychology, but the strong fairy tale echoes throughout the story provide hints to the characters' inner lives.

Temptation and disobedience figure strongly as themes in "In at the Birth". As in such tales as "Bluebeard", there is an alluring secret that coaxes Miss Efoss into action. The Dutts themselves are a mystery. Mr. Dutt is "on the secret list . . . forbidden to speak casually about his work" (p104). He issues a warning to avoid the child's room, much as Bluebeard warned his new wife that under no circumstance is she to enter his locked room. Miss Efoss is accepting of these strictures at first. Only the possibility that she has slipped into a "fantasy world" (p108) of dementia moves her to break the injunction against going into the forbidden room. She is terrified to find not the baby she expects, but an old man near death. However, Miss Efoss cannot confront the Dutts about what she sees in the room, as it would prove her betrayal. Her later conversation with Mr. Dutt emphasizes the mystery at the heart of her interactions with them: "I believe one is not meant to understand. The best things are complex and mysterious. And must remain so" (p111). Trevor leaves Miss Efoss's thoughts about what she has seen in the forbidden room in the realm of speculation. This understated bit of dialogue suggests that

Miss Efoss accepts what she has seen, though she is not exactly sure whether the Dutts are doing something sinister. The close correlation between "Bluebeard" and "In at the Birth" establishes a sinister undercurrent. Birth and death are linked in the Dutts's forbidden room. Miss Efoss's return to the Dutts then, is both a birth and a death. In the Bluebeard story, several unlucky brides are punished with death for entering a secret room. In "In at the Birth", Miss Efoss readily accepts her moribund return to an infantile state in the Dutt house. In both tales, the protagonist is issued a command they must disobey. The price of surrendering to temptation is death.

Trevor's fundamentally pessimistic view on life and death casts "In at the Birth" as a cautionary tale. Not only does it illustrate the dangers of giving in to curiosity, it suggests the extremes to which desire can push people. Mr. Dutt tells Miss Efoss "the longing for a child is a strange force" (p111). The lengths to which the Dutts go to fulfill this desire fall into the realm of the grotesque. The deceptions they perpetrate leave a sense that Miss Efoss has been manipulated somehow into returning to them. This ambiguity is carefully created through the flatness of Trevor's characters. In this way, the story itself becomes a tempting mystery for the reader to solve.

As Trevor follows the formula of fairy tale in "In at the Birth," I patterned the story "A Floating World" on Hans Christian Andersen's familiar "The Little Mermaid." This mermaid is not a supernatural creature, however, but a human being born without feet whose strength is in swimming. I purposely left the characters unnamed in order to create a distancing effect similar to Trevor's which would allow the characters to fit into the fairy-tale tone of the story. The dialogue is rendered indirectly, without quotation marks, in order to establish a narrative reality in which the narrative voice carries the authority to make the grotesque plausible. This story arose from my interest in what I had perceived as the subtext of "The Little Mermaid," namely, that love leads to dissolution. Andersen's Little Mermaid endures a painful existence in order to briefly spend time with a human she has fallen in love with.

This story is often cited as a tragic tale of doomed love. One of the enduring possibilities for the fairy tale in fiction is the exploration of alternative role and outcomes that question the gender biases of traditional tales. It seems that in many fairy tales, to be female is to suffer a fate controlled by outside forces. I wondered what would happen to The Little Mermaid if she rejected her fate. In my story, I made the love interest and the person who gives the Little Mermaid legs the same person. The surgeon remakes the protagonist of "A Floating World" in an image that fulfills his own needs. In Andersen's tale, the Little Mermaid endures the sensation of intense pain in order to have human form. My story keeps this element, but emphasizes the protagonist's self-determining nature. As the protagonist approaches the moment of her marriage to the surgeon, the pain she has endured to inhabit a the body her lover has crafted become overwhelming, until she decides to discard the remade body "as if her body had been a heavy dress, as if she had gladly unzipped it and wriggled her way out." The story is less concerned with a detailed depiction of the protagonist's psychological point of view than it is with presenting a sort of fable. The protagonist does dissolve at the end of the story, a distorted magical event, but does so of her own. The exaggerated actions of the characters operate in a world that is a distorted reflection of reality. I chose to use the story's title as my thesis title to emphasize that my fiction takes place in a world that is just slightly askew from recognizable reality.

In Margaret Atwood's short story "Bluebeard's Egg"—in which a woman learns that her husband has been carrying on a secret affair—the fairy tale becomes a conscious filter through which the protagonist, Sally, relates to the world. Atwood confines the reader to Sally's point of view, but allows for some distance in which to assert a storyteller's voice. Initially, Sally sees her husband Edward as a simple two-dimensional character as in a fairy tale:

Because Ed is so stupid he doesn't even know he's stupid. He's a child of luck, a third son who, armed with nothing but a certain feeble-minded amiability, manages to make it through the forest with all its witches and traps and pitfalls and end up with the princess, who is Sally, of course (p110-111).

Her perception of Edward's innocence colors her characterization of other women as "witches" (p110) and "sirens" (p115). Sally casts herself in the role of Ed's protector, viewing herself as "an angel . . . bringing him food" (p126). She warns him about other women:

They think you're delicious. They'll gobble you up. They'll chew you into tiny pieces. There won't be anything left of you at all, only a stethoscope and a couple of shoelaces (p123).

Atwood here exploits the imagery of child-devouring witches from tales such as "Hansel and Gretel" to emphasize Ed's innocence but also to show how Sally's perceptions are informed by the conventions of the fairy tale. The course in "Forms of Narrative Fiction" that Sally is taking gives Atwood a framework of stories through which Sally attempts to understand her reticent husband. Ed is handsome and successful, therefore he appears virtuously simple to Sally. The distance between Sally and the narrator allows Atwood to use this imagery without making it overtly sentimental.

"Bluebeard's Egg" contains several allusions to fairy tales. While the Bluebeard story is recounted directly in the story, in a technique similar to Munro's tale within a tale, other tales appear in passing. The story of a wizard who gives a young woman an egg, a key and a command not to enter a forbidden room creates a vehicle for Sally to consider her relationship. In the Bluebeard tale, three women undergo this test. The first two are punished with death when curiosity overwhelms them and they enter the forbidden room—discovering an execution chamber of such shocking horror that they drop the egg into a basin of blood, ensuring their transgression will be discovered. The third heroine, however, has the sense to tuck the egg away safely before exploring the forbidden room. Once inside, she reassembles her predecessors and hides them. The wizard returns and, believing the protagonist to have obeyed his orders, promises to marry her. As Sally recounts this story, she attempts to fit her life circumstances into the tale, musing: "Ed isn't Bluebeard: Ed is the egg. Ed Egg, blank and pristine and lovely" (p133).

These stories allow Atwood to insert familiar points of reference that express Sally's interior world. She sees Ed as "a puzzle" (p127), their house as "ice" (p127), echoing the "Snow Queen" tale popularized by Hans Christian Andersen. Atwood writes: "If she should ever solve it, if she should ever fit the last cold splinter into place, the house will melt and flow away . . ." (p127). In the original fairy tale, this action breaks the Snow Queen's evil spell. In Atwood's story, to break the spell would destroy Sally's domestic life. This suggests that Sally is, in part, willfully unaware of Ed's complexity. Atwood compares Ed's self-containment to the tale of "Sleeping Beauty":

His obtuseness is a wall, within which he can go about his business, humming to himself, while Sally, locked outside, must hack her way through the brambles with hardly so much as a transparent raincoat between them and her skin (p111).

Here Atwood reverses gender roles, casting Sally as the rescuer and Ed as the innocent victim. These set roles only heighten the drama once Sally discovers that her concept of Ed is entirely wrong. Atwood's use of these tales illustrates the common virtues of the fairy tale protagonist. As Sally sees Ed, he is guileless, simple, his fundamental goodness expressed in a handsome face. As in Trevor, Sally witnesses something she should not see—Ed touching her friend Marylynn. When Ed breaks out of the role Sally has assigned to him, her entire view of the world is threatened. The one-dimensional figures of the fairy tale are turned around to refute the idea of simplicity. In joining several fragments of fairy tales, Atwood builds up to the inevitable discovery, much like the unlucky discovery of Bluebeard's wife, that reaches a darker place, full of sinister potential. The violence hinted at in Atwood is more psychic than physical. The figures of the fairy tale are utilized to come to a psychological truth about the secrets people conceal.

In the stories discussed here, the fairy tale appears as a gateway to a world full of violence, grotesque figures and danger. These stories reach beyond the simplistic view that fairy tales are moral instruction for children. In giving their own takes on the fairy tale, each of these authors taps into a familiar psychic landscape. Like folktales, mythology and other ancient forms of wisdom, the fairy tale expresses much more than it appears to on the surface. These forms continue to enchant. Fairy tales offer a rich symbolic language. To the writer, the potential for recycling these stories is nearly infinite. The exaggerated world of the fairy tale is one in which I can focus on moments of strangeness that slip beyond the bounds of realist fiction.

Works Cited

Atwood, Margaret. *Bluebeard's Egg: Stories.* Anchor Books. New York: NY. 1983.

Bettelheim, Bruno. *The Uses of Enchantment.* Alfred A. Knopf Inc. New York: NY.
1975.

Carter, Angela. *The Bloody Chamber, and Other Stories.* New York: Penguin, 1993.

Morner, Kathleen et al. *From Absurd to Zeitgeist.* NTC Publishing Group. Chicago: IL.
1997.

Munro, Alice. *Selected Stories.* Vintage Books. New York: NY. 1997.

Trevor, William. *The Collected Stories.* Penguin Books. New York: NY. 1992.

Acknowledgements

Thanks go to Monica Best, Marta Ney, John Best and David Slonim.

I would also like to thank all the people whose care and critiques helped make this book possible, especially Susan Hubbard, Toni Jensen, Darlin' Neal and Pat Rushin.

Karen Best is a bitter Goth masquerading as a nerdy bookworm. She holds an MFA in fiction from the University of Central Florida and her work has appeared in *Our Stories*, *ETC*, and *Filament Magazine*. Early exposure to the paranormal, mythology, fairy tales and Edgar Allen Poe has left her with an abiding interest in dark stories and dressing entirely in black. Karen blogs on Gothic aesthetics at www. LashesAndStars.WordPress.com. She lives in Florida with her obliging husband and several cats.

www.KarenDBest.com